Maple Dale

MaryAnn Myer
April 18, 1999!

Maple Dale

MaryAnn Myers

LIGHTHOUSE
Literary Press, Inc.
Chesterland, Ohio

Lighthouse Literary Press, Inc.
P.O. Box 421
Chesterland, Ohio 44026

First Edition
10   9   8   7   6   5   4   3   2   1

Publisher's Cataloging-in-Publication

Myers, Maryann.
    Maple Dale / Maryann Myers. — 1st ed.
    p. cm.
    LCCN: 98-94135
    ISBN: 0-9668780-1-9

    1. Riding Schools—Fiction.   2. Ghost stories, American   I. Title

PS3563.Y442M37 1999   813'.54
                      QBI98-1585

*Maple Dale is dedicated to Cindy Joy,
my sister in life and dear friend.
And to our mom.*

Leah Oliver was never considered for adoption,
nor was she ever temporarily fostered. Perhaps that was her fault.
Apparently she was lost from the beginning.

-One-

*I*T WAS EARLY on a Saturday morning when Klaus Bukener told Leah he'd decided to sell Maple Dale. And oh, the look in her eyes. It would break your heart. Maple Dale was the only real home she'd ever had.

"Intact? As a riding establishment?"

Klaus belched. "I don't know. I'm not sure. It depends on how I can get the most money."

"I can't believe this," Leah muttered. "Why?"

"Why? Because this place's a headache and I'm tired of it. I'm tired of the whole damned thing."

"But what about the kids? The students?"

"They're not your kids, why do you care?" Klaus said, rather enjoying himself. "I doubt they care about you."

Leah grew quiet for a moment, wondering. "But what about your father? How's he going to feel about this?"

"Dad's senile, he doesn't even know what day it is. I should've known he was crazy when he built this place. What a dreamer."

Leah tried to swallow the lump forming in her throat. "What are you going to do with the horses?"

"I don't know. I haven't thought that far ahead. But it doesn't surprise me that you would."

And that was the beginning, a seeded fate. Maple Dale was on the market for nine months. During that time, Leah watched a slew of prospective buyers come and go. But as time also allowed, her Monday and Wednesday students were now accomplishing two-foot fences, and her Tuesday group had brought home three high-point trophies.

Klaus had become a regular now too and was constantly under-foot. Today when he showed up, Leah was listing horses to be shod on the blackboard in the barn. As usual, he started complaining.

"Damn, this place stinks! How can you stand it? It smells like horse shit!"

Leah gave him barely a glance. "That's because there seems to be a lot of it around lately."

Klaus made a face. He loved her sarcasm. "Well, I finally unloaded the place."

The chalk dropped from Leah's hand, shattering into tiny white fragments of dust at her feet. "Did you get what you wanted?"

"Not quite. But then again, I may get more. And you're not going to like this." He stepped closer, wanting to relish her torment. "I'm going with a developer."

"What?" Leah gasped, looking at him.

"A developer. I'm tired of waiting around. I've got to unload now while the old man's still alive."

Leah stared. "Is this final?"

"No, not yet." Perhaps if she appealed to him. Just perhaps. "I made a counter offer and should hear later today." But Leah made no such appeal. She just turned away. "Leah!" He'd expected at the very least some sort of argument. She disappointed him. "You'll find something else. Who knows, maybe you'll get on with a real life now."

His feeble attempt at compassion was wasted. Leah was already at the far end of the barn and could hear nothing now but the loud roar between her ears.

Later that evening, as she sat in her favorite chair with her cat, Phoenix, curled up on her lap, and Shad, her black Labrador, at her feet, she made a promise. A vow. If Maple Dale was going to be sold to a developer, it would be over her dead body.

The next morning the proposed deal became final. After that, the weeks passed as quickly as the days. Whenever Leah would glance at the clock on the arena wall, it seemed as if the hands on the dial were mocking the swiftness of time. Several of the horses had already been shipped and the remaining would soon follow.

She shuddered at the thought, then reminded herself, "But this is Tuesday," her favorite day of the week, and smiled. She propped her feet on her tack trunk and tilted her chair back so she could look out the observation window into the arena.

On any other day, passive students were bussed in as part of their school curriculum. Maple Dale became a horseback day-care then, and Leah, the head baby-sitter. But on Tuesdays, only the kids who wanted to be there came, and they were full of enthusiasm. They had a goal. They wanted to be equestrians.

Don't get me wrong. It wasn't that Leah didn't like the other students, she did, even the rotten ones, because after all somebody had to. But these past few weeks, the students on Tuesdays, the eager ones, had become her focus. They were her joy, and they were her escape. And it was through them, through their enthusiasm, that she was able to forget, albeit for only one day a week, the eventual demise of Maple Dale.

Her mind wandered. "Be careful, Bethann, Persian Son is especially ornery today. Yes, yes, George, you tack Plisky One. Of course, who else. Sue, you get Lady. Jennifer, you have Barney." She was thinking ahead, anticipating. Jennifer's going to smile a smile full of braces and bands. George will be making fun. Sue's going to be chewing gum and snapping bubbles until told to spit it out, she'd complain and complain. And Bethann, shy, shy, Bethann, will walk silently into the tack room, keeping everything to herself. She knew them all so well, their habits, particularly Bethann. So honest. So sweet. And to catch a glimpse inside her quiet world on occasion, seemed almost like a wish granted without the asking.

One such moment came as Leah was passing Persian Son's stall and overheard her talking to him. She had him tacked and ready for class and was telling him the highlights of her day. What she was saying was of no particular importance, nonsense actually, yet Leah couldn't help but stop and just stand there in awe. Bethann was stroking his forehead ever so gently and she was whispering. A motion as delicate as a breeze, a sound barely heard.

As soon as she realized she was being watched though, the magic ended and her self-consciousness returned. But Leah would never forget that moment, ever. Because in the three years she'd known Bethann, that was the first time she'd ever heard her speak without stuttering.

Bethann was what most people would call a born rider. And while Leah scoffed at the possibility of anyone being *born* a rider, knowing it took years and years of schooling and hard work to become accomplished, even she had to marvel at Bethann. The fundamentals, yes, they were learned, and she'd taught them to her. But the way she could command a horse to bend, and almost bow with obedience, came from somewhere else. A gift perhaps.

Leah glanced at the clock on the arena wall, and since there was time, decided to go home for a moment. This would be Leah's seventeenth year at Maple Dale. She'd come there straight from the orphanage upon answering an ad in the paper for a live-in groom, and was now the respected headmistress. She'd moved twice, going from a small apartment on the second floor of the Century Home that graced the hill just beyond the arena, to a not-so-small one on the first floor. And with her promotion, given to her proudly by the senior Klaus Bukener five years ago, she now lived in the main apartment at the front of the house. She loved it there. She could see everything coming and going, and at night when there was no activity, she could hear the horses. That's how close they were.

Phoenix greeted her with an arched back and a full stretch. Shad, barely lifting his head, simply sighed, though his tail was thumping. Leah smiled, remembering the day she found him. Wet, much too young, and looking like a skinny fur ball with Sasquatch feet, he was thirteen now, his zest having long since given way to arthritis, soft food, and these heavy, heavy sighs.

"I have to check the stove," she told them, as if they could understand. "I was worried I might've left it on. I thought I checked it, but I want to make sure." She could see it was off, but still bent down and sniffed, and satisfied then, started back across the room.

Shad thumped his tail again. "We'll go for a walk later," she assured him. "And don't worry, I'll get you back up the stairs." There were only four, but they were steep, and he'd been having trouble with them of late.

As she walked to the arena and glanced down the road, a chill came over her. As if it had happened just yesterday, she remembered the morning Handsome Sam and Whitchit broke the pasture fence and ended up on the road. The worst time of day. All those cars. She could even hear the screeching of the tires. He struggled so to stand afterwards.

She shivered, forced the painful memory from her mind, and walked faster, refusing to look back. Do something. Do something. She decided to double check the blacksmith's list, where for a second, standing there, she thought she heard Klaus's voice. But when she turned, a wretched pain shot through her side, and he was gone. A strangeness of thought came over her then. And a feeling, a feeling of being smothered. Then darkness, as if someone had covered her with a heavy blanket. A blanket as fragrant as a flower bed, forcing her to the ground.

She lay motionless now with her face against the cold cement, unnerved by her shortness of breath, and wished she could get out from under the weight of the flowers. She could see into the tack room, but it seemed strange. It was dark and empty. Everything gone.

She raised her head as high as she could to look down the aisle, where horses would nicker and nod at the slightest urging, thinking if she could get them stirred, help would come. But the stalls were empty too.

"Oh my God!" she gasped. "The horses!" She had to find them, and forced herself to her knees. There was a pounding in her ears, a pounding and a fluttering. She tried to stand, but another pain gripped her, doubling her over. Such pain. As gurgling sounds bubbled deep in her throat, her jaw stiffened.

She closed her eyes, but only for a moment, and had to struggle with her moist lashes to open them. Her arms were rigid at her sides. She had to force them to bend so she could brace herself. Outside, and getting louder as they approached, were geared-down machines vibrating the earth. The sounds were familiar, that of the busses.

"Finally." No longer concerned about anything now but welcoming the students, she went out to greet them, and felt like she was floating, suspended only inches above the ground as she forced her legs to move, one in front of the other.

It wasn't the busses though. It was construction and excavating equipment, large bus-yellow tractors, clang-clanging their way up the incline with the engines straining. The drivers didn't see her. They passed right over where she stood. And when she turned, with her fists raised to brandish them, she saw the charred ruins of her home, still smoldering.

Somewhere deep in the woods a frightened tabby cat was in hiding, and miles away, an aged Labrador was being helped back into his kennel bed.

You see, there were no busses due to arrive. No students. No equestrians. Yes, it was Tuesday. August 21st, 1988 to be exact. But Leah Oliver was dead. She'd died a week ago, today.

-Two-

Growing up in an orphanage wasn't all that bad, Leah would always reply when asked. It just wasn't that good. She kept that part to herself. In fact, she had pat answers for everything concerning her motherless life, and her expression never betrayed otherwise.

Leah had settled on a plain, simple life, and was frugal to say the least. She never squandered money on useless cosmetics or trendy clothing, never once paid to have her hair cut, let alone styled, and could assemble all her toiletries in half a shoe box. She wore the same style clothing every day of her adult life, beige ratcatcher shirt, tan breeches and field boots. Her only accessory, was a woven belt. At night, regardless of the season, you'd find her in a flannel night-gown and knitted slippers, and only at night, would you ever see her long hair unbraided. She was impeccably groomed at all times and always appeared to have just stepped from the shower, smelling fresh, and with hands as soft as seasoned leather.

Her apartment was furnished simply, though certainly not lack-ing in taste. Two wingback chairs, an oak table, a plaid muslin

Queen Anne loveseat, and a brass bed. She was methodical in the care of her possessions, used a vegetable oil soap for her furnishings, a pine cleaner for her bathroom, and trusted her clothing only to the gentleness of Ivory Snow.

The weeks leading up to Leah's death would link her eternally to the finality of the Maple Dale equestrian program. But the real depth of her suffering couldn't have been imagined as she followed her daily routine, because she never once planned for the day that it would end.

The advanced class was in progress and four aspiring equestrians were schooling their horses through the cavalletti; poles strategically arranged to pace a horse's stride. They'd been instructed to trot through then break into a canter, proceed to the in-and-out set of jumps, on to the artificial brick wall, and after that, to trot and come back through the cavalletti.

Bethann had her head in the clouds and her hands full, but managed under a tight rein to hold Persian Son until the final cavalletti, which he took sloppily, scattering poles in all directions.

"Bethann! Bethann!" Leah scolded. "What the hell was that? Come on! Had those been fences, do you know where you'd be right now? I'll tell you! On the ground! Now collect him and do it again!"

Bethann rarely made an error or misjudgment. Her instincts were uncanny. Had she not been so preoccupied with the sale of Maple Dale, the cavalletti would've still been in place and, Persian Son, on the muscle and all, would have proved no match for her skillful hands. But she was the one student most affected, and her mother's role as real estate agent for the developer, only caused additional anguish. Maple Dale had been a haven for her, and Leah, her best friend.

Leah rearranged the poles, and this time Bethann, with Persian Son on the bit, maneuvered it fluidly. "Yes! Yes! Yes! Much better! Good! Now walk!" Leah swept her hand to include the entire class. Instantly, simultaneously, stirrups were dropped and reins relaxed.

A chorus of soothing words echoed sighs of relief as riders let down with their horses.

It had been an especially grueling session with at least half of it spent at a trot, posting without stirrups, a schooling practice every student dreaded, with thigh muscles burning in agony. But a necessary one nonetheless.

"How else," Leah had said more times than one would care to count, "can you expect your muscles to develop, with control that will become instinctive, second nature, and respond naturally in one with the horse, in perfect balance, but to practice, over and over." Her students knew it by heart, word for word, and often were mouthing it along with her. "Over and over."

Klaus was sitting at her desk when she walked into her office. "Nice class," he said, folding his arms across his midriff.

"They're good students," Leah replied, a matter-of-fact statement sounding more like one given on a deathbed.

Klaus made a face. "Now don't start that again. Those kids'll do just fine without Maple Dale."

"I'm sure they will." Leah sat down on the cot across from him and raised her hand when he started to say something else. "I know, don't tell me. And so will I."

Klaus puffed out his chest and leaned back in the chair to look directly at her. He always liked looking at her when she used this tone. He leaned back too far though, lost his balance, and nearly tipped over before he caught himself. His face turned beet red. "Did you get any offers?"

Leah sighed. "Two."

Klaus turned, furious with himself for almost falling, and tried to look preoccupied with some papers on her desk. "Did you decide on one?"

"No." She didn't want either.

"Hmph." Klaus drew a breath, paused deliberately, and faced her again to unload the blow. "Well, you'd better decide soon. Because in less than two weeks, not only will you be jobless, you'll be home-less as well."

"What? Why so soon? I just talked to Bethann's mother this morning, she says they haven't sold one lot yet."

"I know." Klaus shrugged. "But the developer thinks, and I agree, they might sell quicker with the old house torn down and a model put up in its place."

Leah's eyes widened. "Torn down? That house is in excellent shape. Why tear it down? It's almost completely restored. My God, Klaus, it's a Century Home. They don't make houses like that any-more."

Her tone irritated him, always the authority. "No, you're right there. And that's why it's got to go. It clashes with the style of homes they plan to build here."

Leah stared off, feeling helpless, helpless and tired. Tired of the arguing and tired of the pain. "Whatever."

Whatever...? Klaus pouted. They'd had many long discussions, bordering on knock-down-drag-out fights the past couple of weeks, and he looked forward to them. Giving up was so unlike her. He wanted that old spark. He wanted fire. He wanted attention.

But Leah was miles away, reliving her visit earlier that day with his father at the nursing home.

"You have a visitor, Mr. Bukener," the nurse said cheerfully, as she showed her into the solarium.

He was sitting in a wheelchair facing the window. When he turned, Leah almost didn't recognize him. His silver hair was white now and unruly, as if he'd just gotten out of bed. His ever-tanned, southern-gentlemanly face and engaging smile, now pale and expressionless.

"If we knew we were getting visitors, we would have put our teeth in, wouldn't we, Mr. Bukener?" the nurse said in an exagger-ated and syrupy tone.

He nodded, but remained expressionless, and Leah wondered why it took a visitor to be allowed one's false teeth.

"Now you be nice to your visitor or I'll have to take you back to your room. And we wouldn't want that, now would we?"

Mr. Bukener shook his head and grinned, looking like an obedient child with his hands clasped in his lap, and the nurse left them alone. For a moment, a very awkward moment, Leah found herself focusing on the room around her, the pale green walls, the tables full of potted plants and empty ashtrays, a television set that was turned off. Two women were seated in wheelchairs on the opposite side, one at a table, the tap-tapping of her tremored hand sounded like a pecking bird. The other stared blankly out the window.

Leah thought of the orphanage, first time in a long time, edged a chair up next to Mr. Bukener, too far away at first then closer, and was just about to sit down, when one of the women let out a scream. Leah jumped with her hands clutched to her chest, darting her eyes from the woman to the doorway, expecting a nurse to come rushing through. But no one came.

The room fell silent. Even the woman who'd screamed seemed unconcerned. Leah cleared her throat and sat back down, trembling inside.

"How have you been, Klaus?"

Mr. Bukener frowned and then squinted. His once sparkling, flirting eyes, were now cloudy and harboring mucous in the corners. "I'm fine."

The woman across the room cried out again, and though this time Leah managed to stay seated, it was a moment or two before she felt calm enough to continue. "I've come to talk to you about Maple Dale."

Mr. Bukener looked surprised. "Maple Dale?"

"Yes." Leah hoped she hadn't made a mistake in coming. "Your son is selling it, and I have to stop him."

The old man worked his gums back and forth. "How can he sell it? Is it his?"

Leah hesitated. "I guess."

Mr. Bukener stared at her.

"He wants to tear down the Century Home and the barns and the arena." Her voice cracked. "All of it. I was hoping you'd be able to get him to change his mind. I know how you loved Maple Dale. I can remember when you were well, how we would ride cross country together..." She trailed off, his eyes had filled with tears, that now trickled down his sunken cheeks.

"I would like to ride. And ride, and ride, and ride. And I would never get down."

Leah swallowed hard. "If you could only get him to change his mind. I'm sure he doesn't need the money. He has other business interests."

The old man nodded slowly.

"I know I have no right to ask this of you, but Maple Dale is my home. I'll beg if I have to. You see..." Her chin quivered uncontrollably as she thought about the students, the horses, her home, Shad and Phoenix. "Maple Dale is important to so many people. You just can't let him sell it."

Mr. Bukener lowered his eyes to his lap, stared for a moment, then started scraping at a scab on the back of his hand. The nurse returned. "Are we having a nice visit?"

"Yes," Mr. Bukener drawled.

Leah looked away in an attempt to gain control of her emotions. When she looked back, Mr. Bukener was nodding. Nodding and nodding and nodding.

"Are you related to our Mr. Bukener?" the nurse asked.

"Uh...no, I'm not," Leah managed to say. "I work for him. Actually I work for his son."

"Oh?" the nurse said, sounding interested.

Leah nodded, glancing at Mr. Bukener, expecting him to say something, but he didn't. This was when she realized he didn't know who she was. She was a complete stranger to him.

She stood up quickly, wanting to run from the room, suddenly feeling as if she didn't know him either. But for some reason, he urged her to stay. "Please don't go," he said, his voice a frail semblance of its once boisterous tone. "Please..."

Leah felt for the chair, unsteadily, and sat back down as the nurse addressed one of the women. "Are we having a nice time in the solarium, Mrs. Kennedy?"

When the woman nodded, saying something in a soft but incoherent voice, Mr. Bukener began nodding again as well. "Maple Dale," he said. "It would be so nice to go there. I could get a horse topped off and..."

Leah found herself nodding right along with him, nodding and nodding and nodding even as the nurse stepped back and started shaking her head.

"*Mister* Bukener! That was *not* a nice thing to do!" She released the lock on his wheelchair. "Now we'll have to go back to your room." On the floor beneath him was a puddle.

Bethann tapped on the office door. "Can I s-s-see y-yyou a minute?"

Leah glanced at Klaus, just a fleeting glance, but one he took rightfully so as an invitation to leave, and did. She knew exactly why Bethann was there, and motioned for her to have a seat.

Bethann remained standing. "I want t-t-to talk to y-yyou about P-P-Persian Son."

Leah smiled sadly and shook her head. "We've been over this, Bethann, and my opinion hasn't changed. It's not a good idea."

"But w-w-why?"

"You know why, we've been over that too. You need a better horse." Bethann's hurt expression had Leah quickly correcting herself. "A *younger* horse, and *not* a school horse."

"Persian Son is n-n-not j-j-just a school horse," Bethann said, her determination to defend him far outweighing her aversion to speaking. She even said it again. "He's n-n-not."

Leah motioned once more for her to sit down and this time waited for her to listen. "Persian Son is a fine horse, yes. Probably one of the finest school horses I've ever seen. But. He's fourteen-years old and has more mileage on him than three horses his age. Frankly, I don't know why he stays so eager, so giving. Most horses would have soured years ago."

Bethann smiled. "That's b-b-because h-he's special."

Leah had to smile herself. She envisioned him romping in the paddock and playfully tossing his mane. "Irregardless, I think you ought to look for a younger horse. A five or six-year old maybe."

"I *w-w-want* Persian Son!"

Leah lowered her eyes to the floor, and looked up shaking her head. "Bethann, come on. We've been over this so many times. Can't you understand?"

"No."

Leah drew a breath and sighed. "You know, between this and my discussions with Klaus, I'm worn out. I don't ever remember being this tired."

"I'm s-s-sorry," Bethann said, apologizing sincerely, but making it very clear she wasn't going to change her mind. "He's the-the horse that I w-w-want. Period!"

Such a stand. Leah smiled a proud smile, and with that, waved her hands in surrender. "All right, all right. I give up!"

"You m-m-mean it?"

Leah nodded. "Yes. I'll talk to your parents about the price."

Bethann jumped up and hugged her tightly.

"Quit! Quit!" Leah scolded, patting her on the back. "You really didn't need my okay on this anyway, you know. You could've gone to Klaus yourself."

Bethann stepped back, beaming. She *did* need her okay. She very much wanted her approval. "Now go on." Leah nudged her toward the door, not wanting her to see how choked up she was getting. "Your ride's probably here."

After Bethann left, Leah went out and sat down on the bleachers overlooking the arena. Only now, sitting there alone, would she admit to herself that she was glad she hadn't been able to convince Bethann otherwise. Because she and Persian Son belonged together. Some things were just meant to be.

Leah smiled.

Bethann was probably the only real friend she'd ever had, and oddly enough, considering how shy she was, it was Bethann who befriended her. Every time she turned around, it seemed Bethann was there, following her, talking to her, then following her some more. "Underfoot," Leah would say. But for some reason, they could relate to each other, and had developed a bond that surpassed one's stuttering while tugging at the roots of the other's desolation.

For the record, Leah herself had never owned a horse. That would have taken a direct commitment, something she wasn't capable of doing. Luckily, Shad and Phoenix, both abandoned and stray, had forced their way into her life, leaving her no choice. Ironically though, there was one horse early on that had tempted her, and more than once for that matter. That horse was Persian Son.

-Three-

CHRISTINE MORRISON thought the opportunity to serve as real estate broker for the Maple Dale development was exactly what she needed. It would be a diversion, a way to immerse herself, to hide, yes hide, not to mention what it could do for her career.

The project's format included nine cul-de-sacs and three streets, the plan calling for a total of one hundred and twelve, three-acre lots. And she'd been so enthusiastic, so elevated, only to be brought crashing down by the death of Leah Oliver and the inevitable effect it had on her daughter Bethann. In the weeks prior to this, she'd been able to distance herself from the reasons she'd spent the last year in therapy; her husband's alcoholism, her daughter's stuttering, and the senseless and archaic feeling that somehow she was responsible for both. During those weeks, she wasn't the poor, poor wife, the last to know, and such a nice person yet. She was busy, busier than she'd ever been, and couldn't hear the things being said everywhere she went. She didn't have the time. Now however, she would, and all because of Leah Oliver.

Richard Morrison, for his part, had long ago given up on any chance that he and Christine could pick up the shattered pieces of their marriage and love each other as they once had. He himself, couldn't forget his own actions the past few years, let alone expect Christine to put his atrocities behind them. But exactly when and how it all began, wasn't something Richard was able to recall. He couldn't remember if he'd turned away from Christine, seeking solace in alcohol and other women, or if it started the other way around. It all seemed so harmless at first, the irony being that Christine was hurt most by his initial swaying, and found that the hardest to forgive. No, Richard knew she would never forgive him, but held on to the hope anyway. After all, she had agreed to let him come back home.

As for Bethann, she couldn't understand why her parents remained apart, or even why they'd drifted in the first place. She was sure they still loved each other, but was equally sure of her mother's inability to compromise. Oh, she was well aware of the reasons behind their separation. It was hardly a secret. But so typical of adolescent reasoning, she wanted it all to go away like a scrape on her knee, and heal without even a scar. She was convinced they could be a family again. As sure as her name was Bethann and as sure as she stuttered it could happen, because it had to. It just had to.

On that Tuesday, a beautiful Tuesday, with the sun shining through tufts of cottony cumulus clouds, Leah horrified her students when they found her in the barn, her face pressed against the cement with her eyes so ghastly. She was so young, people would then say. So young and with so much life ahead of her. But they didn't know her. Hardly anyone did. Time, time seemed so important. But the exact time of her death couldn't be determined, though the cause was indisputable. Leah had died of massive heart failure.

Klaus had barely hung up the phone from the call about his father, when he received the one about Leah. Things happened quickly after that. The Century Home was burned to the ground, compliments of the volunteer fire department. Two of the barns were torn down, their siding sold at a premium. Trees gave way to chain saws. The arena now housed construction equipment. And the offices had been taken over by Walter Pugent, Maple Dale's developer.

The Friday following Leah's death, Richard Morrison received a phone call from a colleague, and that evening at home, gave Christine and Bethann the news. Bethann had been named in Leah's will.

Tears filled Bethann's eyes when her father just mentioned Leah's name. He reached for her hand to comfort her. "Honey, the worst is over. Losing someone is never easy, but I promise you, time will ease some of the pain."

When Bethann nodded, dabbing at her eyes, her father continued. "Apparently she had no family, and has left her entire estate to you."

Christine swallowed hard. "What's in it?"

"We won't know until we meet with James Howell, but he alluded to it being her furniture and personal things. Some riding equipment. And oh, the best part." He hesitated, smiling. "Her cat and her dog."

Christine's face went blank, which was typical of her when she was trying to master her thoughts. "I didn't know she had a dog."

Bethann nodded. "She d-d-did. His name is S-S-Shad."

Christine cringed. "Is he small?"

"No. He's a L-L-Lab."

"And the cat?"

"A l-l-little tabby. It was a s-stray."

"Wonderful," Christine said softly, glancing at Richard. "Just wonderful."

Richard nodded, looking quite sincere while smiling inside, something he'd perfected over the years. "The reason James called rather than notify us by mail, was the uniqueness of the will. It seems Leah had it structured to cover any unknown inheritance which may occur from her biological parents, which took some foresight on her part, I might add. Probating this is going to keep him busy for a while." He paused. "Anyway, according to him, she expressed an urgency for her pets, mainly the dog because of its age.

Across town, Klaus Bukener was being addressed by none other than John Smith, distinguished senior partner of Smith & Smith, Attorneys at Law. "The contents of the will and the way it was written, prevented me from telling you this any earlier."

Klaus threw his hand up. "Bullshit!"

John Smith sighed. "The fact remains, that your father made provisions for one Leah Oliver."

Klaus folded his arms high on his chest and stuck his chin out like a playground bully. "Yeah, well she's dead, so it doesn't make any difference."

John Smith felt the hair bristle on the back of his neck. He didn't like Klaus, and doubted if anyone did. "Leah Oliver is dead?"

Klaus sneered. "Dead as a doornail. She died the same day as the old man."

John Smith sat back. The senior Klaus Bukener had been his friend, a good friend, and a shrewd businessman, but most of all, a good man. How in the hell did he end up with a son like this?

"So," Klaus gloated. "So much for ruining my plans."

"Don't be too sure of that. If she has heirs..."

"Heirs! Ha! She had nobody! She only needed herself! Don't you see? I win!"

John Smith rose slowly from his chair. "That'll be for the courts to decide. And if their decision is in Leah Oliver's favor and she has heirs, they will inherit one third of Maple Dale. Now if you'll excuse me."

Leah couldn't understand why the back barns were torn down, why her house burned, or how it was she could sleep in the woods during a rainstorm, without getting wet.

She'd been so happy to find Phoenix, but wondered where Shad was. Making her way past the smoldering remains of her home to find him, she suddenly became fatigued and laid down to rest. Phoenix curled up on her lap, purring, as she drifted off. A car pulled up then and parked next to the arena, only yards away.

Christine gathered her things, got out, and walked toward the office. At the door, she thought she heard someone behind her. She looked around, but no one was there, so she went inside.

Walter greeted her with a cheerful, "Hi!"

Christine smiled and walked past him to her desk, then straight to the coffee pot. They'd decided to set up offices right at Maple Dale, and had settled into a routine of working well together.

Walter looked up as she sat down. "Can you believe all the fuss in the papers about the old house?"

Christine sipped her coffee, and nodded. "Yes. I can."

Walter frowned. "Traitor." When Christine merely shrugged, he went on. "I just got a call from the Historical Society. And boy, you want to talk about getting reamed out."

Christine sympathized, but not with him. "I think that was to be expected. Personally, I still don't see why it had to be destroyed. It was a beautiful structure."

Walter scratched his head with a pencil eraser. "It wasn't my idea, it was Klaus's. Besides, it *was* old."

Christine took another sip of coffee. "Yes, and if it fell down one day, that would be okay. But to destroy it, to burn it down no less, ruffles the feathers of every historian in sight."

"Yeah well, it's done, so we might as well just forget about it."

Christine nodded, true, and was quiet for a moment. "Bethann'll be by later."

Walter smiled. "Is she coming to see the progress?"

"No, she's going to look for the cat that ran away. The one that belonged to Leah Oliver."

"Ah yes. *The* Leah Oliver."

Christine scowled. "Why do you say it like that?"

"No reason, really. I just know I wasn't one of her favorite people."

"Is it any wonder? Come on." Christine found herself on the defense again, first on behalf of the Society and now Leah. "She didn't want this development. She fought it with everything she had."

"I know." Walter laid his pencil down and sat back. "But still. I came up here once when she was giving a lesson, right out there." He pointed to the arena. "She just glared at me, *I mean glared,* and if looks could kill." He rolled his eyes. "I only met up with her one time after that. She was walking her dog up on the north end where all the jumps are. And she wouldn't even look at me. A couple of days later she was dead. She seemed so young too."

"She was the same age as me," Christine said. "But again, in all fairness, I don't think you saw her best side. It was just the project, and consequently, you. Actually she was well liked, especially by her students."

Walter shook his head. Leah's story was sad, but life goes on. He picked up his pencil. "Here, come see, I'm rerouting the street on the southwest corner. We'll be able to save more trees that way and make Bill happy. Which reminds me, I was up there this morning and saw a cat. A small gray one."

"Really? That could be it."

"What kind of shoes do you have on?" Walter asked, leaning to look.

"Loafers. Why?"

"Let's take a walk up the hill. Come on. That way I can point out the re-routing to you. It just may help in selling the lots up there. Bringing the road in through the other way like Bill suggested gives it a whole new dimension."

"All right. Maybe we'll see the cat."

As they walked around the back of the arena to the path that led to the cross country course, Leah watched. Phoenix had long since removed himself from her lap and was abound with his new freedom, meandering about the grounds like a stalking hunter. He scaled a tree quickly, but his skill proved inferior to his enthusiasm, and he lost his balance. A fall was imminent as he held on frantically with his front claws, hind legs dangling. Leah rushed to his rescue, scolding him and comforting him as she reached up and pulled him to her chest. By the time she put him down and turned, Walter and Christine were gone.

Bethann had Persian Son almost cooled out when her father arrived. He was hoping to get there in time to watch some of her lesson and see how she was adjusting to a new stable and a horse of her own, but he'd been delayed in court. When she saw him she waved, signaling she'd only be a few minutes.

"What?" he said, cupping his hand to his ear. "What did you say?"

Bethann rolled her eyes and made a face. He always did things like this. "Dad..."

"Yes? You were saying?"

Bethann laughed. "Ten m-m-minutes."

"Good." Richard nodded, smiling, and walked over to talk to her instructor while she finished up.

If you were to ask Bethann, she'd say her dad was the best dad in the world. And she'd mean it. She idolized him, even if he did insist she speak when she'd rather wave, nod, smile, frown, or otherwise avoid having to say anything. In her eyes he could do no wrong, which made the fact that he was maybe the world's worst husband, such a puzzle to her.

"I picked up the dog," Richard said, as they started outside.

"Is he in t-t-the car?"

"No, I took him home. I wasn't sure if he liked being in a car. He's probably confused and scared. I thought it would be better just to take him home."

Bethann agreed and got in the front seat. "Think M-M-Mom'll like him?"

Richard smiled. "I doubt it."

"But he's a n-n-nice d-d-dog."

Richard smiled again and started the car. "He seems like it. Who knows, maybe he'll grow on her. You want to stop for a milk shake?"

Bethann nodded.

"What's that? What did you say?" Richard poised an attentive ear and began singing, "Said the little shepherd boy to the mighty king, do you hear what I hear...?"

Bethann laughed. "Oh, Dad!"

"Yes...?"

"Yes, I w-w-would like a m-m-milk shake."

Richard gave her a gentle shove. "Me too."

They stopped at Dairy Queen then headed for Maple Dale where for a good hour and a half, they combed the grounds for Leah's missing cat. It was nowhere to be found, and getting dark, so they left, picked up a pizza for dinner as planned, and arrived home just before Christine.

Shad had sniffed and inspected every inch of the house and finally settled on the rag rug in the den, apparently claiming it as his own as he stretched out on his side and heaved a heavy sigh.

"He'll probably leave hair everywhere," Christine said, scowling as she watched Richard pet him.

Richard winked at Bethann with his head down, and nobody said anything for a moment.

"Do you th-think he m-m-misses Leah?"

Richard shrugged, still petting him. "Oh, I guess so. Dogs get pretty attached to people."

"But he d-d-doesn't act l-like it. He doesn't even look when I s-s-say her name. L-L-Leah. L-L-Leah."

Christine, using her fork, cringed with each anchovy she plucked from her pizza. "Maybe he's hard of hearing. He *is* old." She hated anchovies, and couldn't understand how Richard and Bethann could eat them. "Besides, if she lived alone like you said, he probably hasn't heard her name that often, if ever."

Richard nodded, agreeing, and Bethann sat back and smiled. It made sense, and it made her feel better. She took a bite of her pizza, looking from her mother to her father, and for a moment, a fleeting moment, it was as if they were a family again. A real family.

-Four-

CURIOSITY AND GREED sent Klaus out to Maple Dale before dawn to ransack through Leah's possessions like an amateur thief. Greed and determination. If she had a will, he was damned sure going to find it. And then he was going to destroy it.

When his frantic search proved futile, he glared at his watch and decided he'd better leave, when suddenly it occurred to him to try one more place. Her tack trunk. "Yes!" Underneath all the neatly arranged bridles, bits, and girths, was an inlaid letter box wrapped in a chamois. He sat down at her desk to pour through the contents.

He tossed the pictures aside and didn't seem to care that they were all of Maple Dale. He dropped a bundle of report cards to the floor and didn't notice that they were in chronological order and that Leah had never once failed to make the honor roll. He wasn't impressed with the numerous little slips of paper signifying all the times she'd donated blood. He got his hands on her legal documents and medical records, and that's all he wanted. "I was right! I knew it! No will!"

Leah didn't know how the arena surface had gotten into the condition it was in, but something definitely had to be done with it before she could set up jumps for the day's class. As she was going for a rake she heard a noise and turned, her hands clutched tightly to her chest as she watched Klaus walk toward the exit. Then she went to work.

Walter and Christine were meeting Bill for breakfast, and as usual, Christine was early, Bill was on time, and Walter was late. The trio when assembled looked somewhat out of place with one another. Walter, tanned and in a pair of faded Levis, gray wool sweater, tweed blazer, elbow patches, and pipe. Christine, pale and blonde, in a gray linen three-piece suit. And Bill, black, and dressed in a crisp, khaki work uniform.

Bill Forbes's charismatic nature hadn't captivated Christine as Walter had promised, his good looks aside. If anything, she was a little afraid of him. He was polite enough and never said anything directly. But right from the start, she got the impression he resented her being on the project with them, and couldn't decide if it was because she was white or because she was a woman. Whatever the reason, he seemed to be deliberately excluding her from most discussions, and at times, acted as if she weren't even there.

Bill was born and raised in a tract of falling-down shacks on the Mississippi River side of the projects in New Orleans where the white people lived, and had worked hard to distance himself from there. An all-around athlete, he was educated by way of scholarships awarded him for the lean, muscular legs of a basketball center, the arms and shoulders of a football tackle, and the drive of a Mack truck. He smiled easily, a broad smile taking over his entire face, and he was slow to anger. But once riled, paths were cleared.

The Maple Dale project was the largest he and Walter had undertaken since they'd formed their partnership. The one that was going to put them on the map, so to speak. But from the onset, the contract they had with Klaus bothered Bill. If they'd had the funds to buy the property outright, it wouldn't have been a consideration. As it was, Klaus was an active voice.

Walter on the other hand, accepted the arrangement without reservation. He loved his work, he lived for it. Whatever he was doing, whether it be eating, driving, or watching television, he never stopped planning, dreaming. He'd jot down ideas on napkins, receipts, his clothing, his hands, anything, and every last detail so he wouldn't forget. Jumping at any new concept or angle that would set his work off from another builder, something as basic as the sign at the entrance to one of his developments became a challenge, and subject to numerous drive-by's from both directions, car first, then a van, and finally a truck, to be sure it was perfect from every angle.

Christine listened with enthusiasm as Walter went over yet another change, allowing for even more of the natural landscape to remain untouched, but Bill grew impatient. He was a doer, not a planner. Give him the sketch and let him go.

"This is all fine," he said, when Walter had finally run down. "But what I'd like to know is, what are we going to do about the vandalism?"

"More?" Walter asked.

Bill nodded. "I stopped by on my way here to check on the crew. The two tractors we left up on the site at the north end wouldn't start."

"Maybe they're just damp," Walter suggested.

"Damp...? You got that right. Someone put water in the gas tanks."

Walter leaned forward. "Are you sure?"

Bill's expression answered that.

"Was there anything else?"

"A few things."

"Could it be somebody on the crew?"

"No." Bill shook his head. "These are strange things, things no one in their right mind would do."

"Could it be kids, fooling around?"

"I don't know. I don't think so."

"What do you mean strange?" Christine asked, making her presence known. "Like weird strange?"

Bill glanced at her, stared at her actually, for a second or two, then shrugged, and Christine clammed up. He was doing it again, ignoring her. But what Bill was really thinking had nothing to do with her, and probably couldn't have been explained anyway. It stemmed from years and years of watching his mother knock on wood and throw salt over her shoulder. Bill was as superstitious as they came. Strange only meant one thing to him. *Strange.*

Richard was scheduled to be in court within the hour and was busy scanning briefs when the intercom buzzed. "Mrs. Morrison to see you."

He hesitated. Christine? Here? "Uh, send her in." He stood up, straightening his tie and smoothing the front of his shirt, and just as quickly felt foolish for doing so. Christine was his wife. Why was he fussing like this? To make an impression? And why did he suddenly feel so giddy? More importantly, why had she come to the office, the first time in over a year?

When Christine entered, smiling faintly, Richard didn't know whether to embrace her, kiss her on the cheek, or shake her hand. He found himself motioning to the chair across from his desk instead.

"Do you have a minute?" she asked.

Richard glanced at his watch. "A few. Why?"

"I want to tell you about the meeting this morning with Walter and Bill." Christine sat down, folded her hands on her lap, and crossed her legs at the ankles. "It seems there are some quirky things going on at Maple Dale." She lowered her already soft voice. "Vandalism."

"Vandalism?"

"Yes. Nobody's there after the work shift, so I guess it was to be expected in one form or another. It's just..." She leaned her head back and sighed. "It's just that I don't want anything else to spoil this. It means so much to me."

Richard nodded. No one knew more than him how much it meant, and also how much she needed it, especially now. Matt said the best thing for both of them at this stage was to keep busy. "What would you like me to do, Christine? How can I help?"

Help? "Um..." Christine stood up, feeling very foolish all of sudden. What *had* she come for? "I just thought I'd tell you what was going on. I uh, I'd better go."

Before Richard could even get up from his chair, she walked out, leaving him to stare at the closed door and wishing just once that he'd say the right thing. His first impulse was to chase after her. Tell me what to say, Christine, and I'll say it. Please. But he knew better. He walked to the window instead, and watched her as she got into her car and drove away.

It was times like these when he wanted a drink the most. Just one. That's all it would take. Just one to prove to himself that he could walk away from it. Because if he could do that, wouldn't it prove to Christine that he would never make the same mistakes again?

He gathered his things, threw them into his briefcase, and left. The courthouse was only two blocks away with more than enough time to get there, yet he practically jogged. Today however, on time, early, or late, made no difference.

Law school professors take great pains to prepare their students for the bureaucratic procedural let down. Nonetheless, it was aggravating. After weeks of preparation, sometimes months of hours logged researching and building a case, an empty feeling was all that came with the sound of the gavel and dismissal. Even when you've won.

Richard walked down the hall, stopped at the water fountain, and looked up when he heard someone call his name. It was James Howell.

"Your secretary said I'd catch you here." He shook Richard's hand warmly. "I've got to meet with you right away. There's a new twist in my client's will."

"You want the dog back?" Richard teased.

James Howell laughed. "No, not hardly." He motioned for Richard to walk with him. "I'm meeting with John Smith in about an hour on it."

Richard wondered what John Smith, semi-retired, but still one of the most prominent attorneys in the area, had to do with the case. "Do you want to share any of this with me?"

James Howell waved over his shoulder and boarded the elevator. "I'll get with you later."

Richard blocked the door from closing. "My daughter'll fight you for the dog," he warned. And they both laughed.

Bill believed in working right along with his crew and had a reputation for being fair, but equally demanding. He hated distractions, delays, or obstacles interfering with his schedule, and wasn't at all pleased with having to drive the equipment back to the arena at the end of the day. But it beat leaving it out in the open and easy prey for the vandals.

He had his men knock off a little before four to allow time for the trip back and manned the largest of the tractors himself. Every so often, an obscenity rose above the diesel engines as they were jostled, rocked, bounced, and at times, almost unseated. The first tractor stopped abruptly just inside the arena, causing a chain reaction.

Bill stood up. "What the hell?"

When the driver motioned inside, Bill got down, grumbling as he came to take a look. There before him were jumps, beautifully arranged sets of red, white, and blue fence posts and standards.

If this was someone's idea of a joke, he wasn't laughing. Adding to this, were the two vandalized tractors behind him, running rough, and vibrating the ground as they spit and sputtered.

"Kill the engines!" he barked, and headed straight for the office. "What the hell's going on?"

Walter and Christine looked up from their desks with puzzled expressions. Bill filled the doorway with his size, and the room with his voice.

"What do you mean?" Walter asked.

"What do I mean?" Bill walked to the window and pointed out. "Who set the jumps up?"

Walter and Christine turned, all the more puzzled now. "I don't know," Walter said.

Bill looked at Christine. "Were they like that when you came?"

She shook her head. "I honestly didn't notice."

Bill threw his hands up, glanced at the clock on the arena wall, swung around, and threw his hands up again. "Shit!"

Bethann came in behind them and sat down quietly on the edge of the bleachers.

"I'm not about to pay time and a half for this! This is ridiculous!"

When Walter nodded, Christine noticed Bethann. "Did you find the cat?" she whispered.

Bethann shook her head.

"What cat?" Bill turned, eyes wide.

"A gray tabby," Christine said, answering for Bethann and going over and putting her arm around her.

"A tiger cat, you mean?" Bill said, indicating its size with his hands. "A little scruffy thing?"

Bethann nodded. "Have you s-s-seen him?"

"Yes," Bill said. He did. But before he could say where, Bethann glanced past him into the arena and got a strange look on her face, one that made Bill's stomach drop. This was the third time today he'd had the same uneasy feeling.

Bethann walked to the window, stared out in disbelief, and turned to her mother. "That's L-L-Leah's course. It's h-h-her schooling c-c-course."

That was enough for Bill, more than enough. He sat down on the bleachers with a sigh, buried his face in his hands, elbows on his knees, and started mumbling to himself.

Christine's voice seemed far away. "Honey, that's not Leah's course."

"Y-Y-Yes it is!" Bethann insisted.

"Want us to move everything out?" one of the workers called from the arena.

Bill looked up and seeing the time, waved and shouted back. "No, go ahead and knock off. I'll park'em." He managed a smile, but it was an effort. He'd seen something earlier in the day on top of everything else that made it impossible for him to toss this off lightly. He got up and started to walk out, but stopped then and looked at Bethann.

"Do you know the distance between those first two jumps?"
She nodded. "Nine and a h-h-half feet."

Bill pulled a tape measure out of his pocket and went to check. He knew she'd be right, doing it more out of hope than doubt, and with that, he climbed aboard the first tractor, gunned the engine starting it, and jerked it forward.

Later that evening over dinner, Bethann told her father all about what had happened. He listened carefully, trying to appear as if he were being told an amusing story, and turned to Christine, fully expecting her to scoff and say Bethann had been exaggerating. But she didn't.

Quite the contrary. "I don't know what to make of it. She says no one knew that course but Leah. That it was a special one."

Richard smiled, watching Christine as she blotted the sides of her mouth with her linen napkin, always the lady, and turned to Bethann. "Now that's silly. If *you* knew the course, then someone else could have."

Bethann shook her head, not the least convinced, and Christine had to agree. "I've tried every possible explanation I can think of. But frankly, Rich, it *is* weird. I mean, think about it. Why would anyone want to set them up anyway? What for? And when?" She folded her hands upon saying this and now waited for Richard to come up with a logical summation, so typical of her.

He remained quiet. She'd called him Rich, something she hadn't done since before they were married. *Richard,* she told him, was more appropriate for success, and had called him that ever since. He wondered if she had any idea how much pressure it was for a kid called Rich to all of a sudden be looked up to as a man named Richard.

"Dad, are y-y-you listening?"

"Yes, I am, honey," he said, with a smile. "Only I'm going to have to think about this for a while." He motioned to the dog. "Take Shad for a walk, he acts like he has to go."

After they'd gone, he turned to Christine. "What do really make of it?"

She shrugged. "I don't know," she said, and paused. "But I'll tell you this, Bill didn't like it. I think he believes her. And you know, I think he's a bit strange himself. He wouldn't let his men move the jumps. He left them as they were and parked the tractors all around them. He said something about leaving them taking the fun away for whoever set them up in the first place, but I don't know."

Richard studied her eyes. "You have to admit it is odd," he said, with a hummed rendition of the theme from The World Beyond.

Christine chuckled and shook her head. "You know what else? Bethann knew the exact distance between each and every jump. Bill kept calling out for her to give him the lengths and parked the tractors from that. She knew them all. It was amazing."

Richard sat back. "Come on, let's not blow this out of proportion. Of course she knows the distances, she probably took the course often enough. And someone else obviously did too."

Christine stood up and started stacking dishes. "You're right, we have to keep this in perspective."

Richard watched her walk away and then come back. "Bethann tells me she didn't see any sign of the cat today either." He handed his plate over, looking up into her eyes. "Maybe he's long gone."

"Oh no, he's there," Christine insisted. "Bill said he saw him."

Richard grew quiet, wondering. "Have you ever given any thought to spirits?"

Christine's eyes widened. "Oh, Richard. Not you too?"

He smiled. "No, I don't think Leah Oliver set the jumps up."

Christine loved his smile. It was that same smile that had melted her resistance one winter night many years ago. The very same smile he had on his face when he said, "I do," back when she believed he did. But now she turned away from it.

Richard swallowed hard, reminded of everything he'd done wrong in a glance. He took a sip of his coffee. "I ran into James Howell today at the courthouse. He says there's more to the Leah Oliver will, something he'll fill me in on when we meet."

Christine sat down slowly. "What do you suppose it is?"

"I don't know. Maybe it has something to do with the infamous cat." He cocked an eyebrow. "Maybe there never was one. Maybe he's just a figment of everyone's imagination."

"Oh, Richard. You don't really think...?"

He laughed. "No, I was just kidding. Honest."

-Five-

THE ANNUAL CROSS COUNTRY EVENT at Maple Dale had always drawn some of the finest horses and riders in Ohio. Klaus Bukener Sr. loved to cross country, and thus, had spared no expense on the design of the course. Leah looked forward to these three days with childlike enthusiasm. Not only did it allow her students to shine among the best, it was always held the first week in autumn, her favorite time of year.

Maple Dale was a myriad of color, glorious as she walked the course searching for rocks, holes, or grooves in the turf, correcting anything that could prove disastrous to a horse's fragile legs. She stood back to admire the view. With her imagination never more vivid, she was astride, feeling the exhilarating spray as she soared over the water jump and bounded across obstacle after obstacle, in one with her horse. A highstrung horse. A horse that stopped suddenly, with nowhere to go, and disappeared right out from under her.

"Oh my God!" she gasped. No wonder. "What happened to the trees? They're gone." She sank to the ground, feeling as desecrated as the earth. The cross country course couldn't be taken without the large oaks to mark the way. She could move fences and rake tanbark.

But a tree? She laid her head down on the moist grass and cried, her tears of frustration turning into sobs.

A workman about fifty yards away stopped to listen for a second and looked around. He asked the man next to him if he'd heard anything. When the man said no, he looked around again, shrugged, and went back to work.

Richard phoned Christine a little after lunch to tell her that James Howell wanted to meet with them.

"Today? I can't. I'm going to be busy here all day. Why can't you just go? You know how I hate all that stuff."

"Sorry, but he insisted on both of us. Plus there's more. John Smith will be coming with him."

"What? Why?"

"I don't know, James couldn't say. But they'd like to meet us out at Maple Dale at four. Will Bethann be there?"

"Yes," Christine said, in a soft, mind-wandering voice. "I'd planned on picking her up from school and bringing her back with me. The cat thing, you know."

"Then I'll see you there."

"Wait! Why out here? That's spooky. Why not at your office, or at the house for that matter?"

Richard listened patiently as she went on and on, a habit of hers that last year would've annoyed him. Today, it amused him. "Maple Dale was her home, remember. Now come on, I've got to go. I'll see you later."

John Smith and James Howell arrived a few minutes early, overwhelming Christine somewhat, as Bethann sat calmly on the top bleacher, oblivious to John Smith's reputation or the magnitude of what it would take to get him involved in a simple will.

When Richard came in, the three attorneys exchanged handshakes, brief comments about the weather and the Bruning trial that had been monopolizing the news, and ultimately, their predictions for the Browns - Steelers game Sunday.

Walter gathered his prints to leave, but Richard urged him to stay. "You might want to be here for this."

James Howell agreed, as did John Smith. "Klaus Bukener Jr. will be joining us as well."

No sooner said and in he came, pouting and crumpling papers as he sat down on the edge of Christine's desk. "Okay, let's get this over with."

John Smith passed an indistinguishable glance in his direction and turned his attention to the others. "I represent the deceased Klaus Bukener Sr. in this matter, and appreciate you meeting with me on such short notice." He paused to make eye contact with each one of them. "I apologize for the vague information I'm about to bestow upon you."

Klaus shifted his weight with a great deal of exaggeration, but was ignored as John Smith continued. "I understand you've been informed of Leah Oliver's wishes to some extent."

Richard nodded, smiling supportively at Bethann.

"Good." John Smith hesitated. "Which brings me to the reason I have asked you all here today. My client made a provision in his will for Leah Oliver."

Richard, Christine, and Bethann looked at one another.

"I am reluctant to disclose this information with the will yet to be probated, but the circumstances warrant it." John Smith focused on Bethann a moment before turning to Richard. "Klaus Bukener Sr. has willed one third of the Maple Dale estate to Leah Oliver."

A hush fell over the room.

"It was bequeathed to her for her years of dedication to the equestrian program, in the hopes that she would keep it alive."

Tears filled Bethann's eyes, prompting Christine to go over and put her arm around her before John Smith proceeded. "Which is obviously why I've thrown procedure out the window here today. Now as to the Maple Dale development project..."

Richard stared, realizing now where this was headed and worrying already about how Christine was going to handle it.

"Informally, I can only advise you to cease operation."

Walter's eyes widened in disbelief.

"And leave the decision as to whether to continue or not, until both wills have been probated."

In the moment of heavy silence that followed this statement, Walter glanced at Christine, who was still comforting Bethann. He shook his head and sighed. And that was that.

James Howell asked if he could see Leah's belongings. Klaus was unsure of the condition he'd left them, agreed reluctantly, and unlocked the storeroom door. It creaked as he pushed it open, and the lights flickered. Not once but twice. And out came a shrieking cat.

Bill had the misfortune of entering at this point. Everyone startled by the cat turned from one direction to the other. The cat bolted across the room in a blur, scurrying across the steel toe of Bill's boot, startling him as well. He mumbled something in Cajun, something low and throaty, frightening in itself. And it was at this precise moment, with a final and unusually load tick, that the clock on the arena wall stopped.

Bethann chose to ride home with her mother, knowing her father would insist she talk. Always stuttering more when she was tired, she pretended to be exhausted from chasing the cat, and knew her mother would spare her the effort.

Christine watched her burrowing down in the seat, and smiled. "Maybe you'll catch him tomorrow."

Bethann yawned dramatically. "Maybe." Not realizing just how tired she really was, she drifted off before they got to the main highway, and was in the barn with Leah.

The two of them were braiding Persian Son's mane for a show, using cinnamon-colored yarn to blend with his liver-chestnut color. Leah was stressing that she should never use yarn that could be seen. Persian Son was a hunter, not a carrousel pony.

Leah led him out of his stall when they were done and hooked him up to the cross ties to tack him. She used her own rolled-leather bridle and her own saddle. The next thing Bethann knew, Leah and Persian Son were moving away from her, backwards. And Leah was whispering, "Never turn your back on a friend. Never..."

Christine nudged her gently. "Hey, sleepy head. We're home." She looked like a little girl sleeping and yet so grown up. "Come on." She nudged her again. "Wake up, or I won't let you out of talking anymore when you think you're pulling one over on me."

Bethann smiled, rubbing her eyes. Shad greeted them at the door, wagging his tail. After the bustle of preparing and eating dinner, Richard suggested they all go for a walk. Christine declined, knowing he'd be able to reach out to Bethann easier if she weren't with them. Besides, lately she'd been feeling pretty weak around him, especially in the evenings. And to give in to him even the slightest would mean she'd forgiven him, something she swore she would never do. She couldn't. Because to forgive him, would mean she'd have to accept some of the blame herself.

Richard and Bethann walked slowly, making sure Shad stayed away from all the flowery bushes, but allowed him to cock his leg on the occasional straggly ones, these and all the light poles they passed. As they walked, they talked about the weather, the air smelling good, like now and after a storm and when the grass was just mowed, and debated over why a dog smelled funny after being outside, why only some birds fly south and others don't, why and how roosters know when to crow, and why fire hydrants were red. Bethann thought they should be blue, and Richard agreed.

On the way back, they came upon Matt Campbell, who was jogging as usual, his favorite pastime. He waved, bobbed around them, checked his watch, patted Shad on the head, and jogged on. Matt, in Richard's opinion, was about as crazy and yet as sane a psychiatrist as he'd ever met. And unrelenting. He was also his best friend.

When they got home, Richard sat Bethann down in the den and asked her to tell him all about Leah, which triggered an instant onslaught of tears. "Go ahead and cry," he said, hugging her gently. "Your mom says it's good to let things out."

Bethann hated to cry, almost as much as she hated to stutter. As a small child, they seemed one and the same. Crying and stuttering. Stuttering and crying. "I th-th-thought this would g-g-get easier, but it's n-not. It's g-g-getting harder."

Richard nodded, helpless to offer anything. What attorney John Smith had laid in her lap would be difficult enough for an adult to handle, let alone a fifteen-year old. Klaus Bukener's father's wish was for Maple Dale to continue its equestrian program. Leah's wish would obviously be the same. And now, both those wishes had been passed on to her.

Bethann pulled away, wiping her nose, and in doing so, smeared mucous across her cheek. Richard smoothed her hair, smiling first, then laughing, and handed her his handkerchief. "Here. Your mother would have a fit if she came down and saw you with snot all over your face."

Bethann sniffled, laughing as well now, and blew her nose. "May I w-w-write about Leah instead of t-t-trying to tell you?"

Richard hesitated. He knew he shouldn't give in and should encourage her to talk no matter how difficult it was, but the pained look in her eyes was more than he could bare. "Okay, but just this once."

Christine had gone up to the bedroom to lie down. With so many things running through her mind, quiet and solitude was all she could handle. She had the radio low, the door shut, and was stretched out on her back, staring at the ceiling. Being alone in the bedroom was something she was used to. She'd agreed to let Richard move back home to try to lead a normal life, for his sake as well as Bethann's. But she hadn't agreed to let him back into her heart, or her bed. No. While Richard fought to control his addiction to alcohol, needing his family to do that, Christine struggled with her own battle, denying his love, one day at a time.

Morning came too quickly for Bethann. She'd been up half the night remembering things about Leah, reliving them in her mind. But when she tried to put them into words, they seemed childish, and she'd find herself starting all over again.

When she'd first met Leah, she wasn't sure she was going to like her, and would never in a million years, forget her first lesson when Leah announced to the rest of the class that she stuttered. She wanted to cry. It seemed so cruel. Kids her own age making fun of her was bad enough, let alone a grown up. It wasn't until the lesson was almost over that she realized how much easier it was getting it out of the way right from the start. At least she didn't have to deal with everyone's surprised looks when she opened her mouth.

Leah had a unique way of introducing all her students. No exceptions. She'd say things like, "Class, we have a new student joining us. His name is Doug, who I understand's been under the direction of Grace Abott." Everyone would boo. "Now, now, let's give him the benefit of the doubt. Elbows in, thank you very much, we'll definitely have to work on that.

"Doug, I'd like you to meet Sue. She's on the bay witch respectively called Lady. Don't watch her hands, she's reaching for the stars. We're working on getting them back down to earth with her glue-tight seat, and one would do well do have her legs over fences. Just don't smile at her or anything. She's approaching puberty and giggles for absolutely no reason whatsoever. It's most annoying.

"Now Bethann over there on the large chestnut used to need a ladder, thank God she finally grew. She has balance galore, just don't get in her way. She stutters and just may run you over before she can yell out a warning. There'll be wrecks everywhere.

"And that's George on the gray. Godawful neck, isn't it? The gray, not George. But if you hear moans, it's probably Plisky. Poor,

poor, Plisky. We have George on a diet, but twice last week we caught him hoarding grain."

If she didn't know anything about the new student, she'd declare that for the next few weeks everybody would be watching and looking for something. "You might as well just show it now," she'd say, which usually brought out the worst in all of them. The laughter that followed sounded like a circus.

Bethann read back over what she'd written, put it in an envelope and on her father's desk, passed on breakfast, and left for school.

Christine munched on a piece of toast originally intended for Bethann, and sipped her third cup of coffee. Shad was asleep at her feet, his occasional sigh a comfort to her for some reason. It seemed odd that he would take to her. She'd never liked dogs and had never had one, not even as a child. If forced to choose one, she probably would have gone for a Poodle or a yapping Yorkshire Terrier, a tiny dog that didn't shed. And he'd be too short to leave nose marks on almost every window in the house. Definitely short.

When she got up for another cup of coffee and sat back down, she couldn't help but smile when Shad curled up again at her feet.

Richard never came down for breakfast, a habit he'd developed when mornings were rough, his breath offensive, his hands shaky, and his eyes painfully red. Even now, up early and each morning a pleasure, he remained in his room until everyone was gone.

Though officially there was no reason for Christine to report to work today, she figured Walter would be an emotional wreck, and decided to go give him some moral support. If nothing else, she could at least reassure him of her determination to keep the project moving ahead.

Shad thumped his tail when she put on her jacket, looked at her with his big brown eyes, and got up slowly and followed her to the door.

"What do *you* want?" Christine said.

His wagging tail shook his whole body.

"You've been out twice already," she told him. He'd done the same thing yesterday. She hadn't given in then and wasn't about to now. She kept her wits, feeling just a little silly talking to a dog, and locked the door behind her. Halfway down the walk, she stopped and went back, peeked in at him and promised to return soon.

"I won't be long. Go take a nap."

Richard heard her leave and came downstairs, poured a cup of coffee, patted Shad on the head, and went into his den with the newspaper tucked under his arm.

The letter from Bethann was on his desk. He chuckled as he picked it up. She'd drawn a smiley face on the front. As he sat down to read it, Shad meandered in and stretched out on the rag rug with a heavy sigh.

Dad,

You asked me to tell you about Leah, so I'll try. Leah was very special to me, and even though she was as old as you and Mom, she didn't seem like it. Sometimes when she'd yell at us, it did. But most of the time, she was just my friend. I think it's because we were alike in lots of ways, not just the riding, but a lot of things. It was as if we didn't have to talk to know what the other one was thinking. She hated the fact that I stuttered almost as much as I do. But she'd never feel sorry for me or anything like that. She would wave her hand and try to get me to talk faster. And most of the time I could. When I couldn't, the look on her face was exactly how I felt.

I've tried to think of ways to tell you about her, and how I feel, but it's hard. I don't know exactly what to say. I can tell you about this one time when a horse I didn't like refused a jump three times and dumped me twice, and how mad he made me. I wanted to quit and felt like crying. But when Leah helped me up and handed me the reins she said some-thing like, your heart is what's going to get you and this beast over that fence. This is not your fault unless you give up. Understand? Now get back up there and get over that jump. And I did.

All of us liked Leah, because she made us feel special in spite of our mistakes. She was always telling you when you did good and you knew she meant it. Because when you did bad she told you that too. That's the way she was.

I've heard these past few weeks that she was nothing but a lonely woman, but I don't think that's true. I'm not saying that I think she was happy being alone, just like I'm not happy that I stutter. But sometimes there's nothing you can do about it. One time I asked her about her saddle and why she didn't have knee rolls or a forward seat, and she laughed. I can close my eyes and see her laughing. She said she preferred things simple. The finest quality, but simple. Then she said something that I didn't really understand then but I think I understand now. She said she liked things plain, because it was what she did best.

I don't know if Leah had a personal life, because she never talked about it. Maple Dale was her life. And if it's possible, I hope we can make sure Maple Dale never forgets her. I know I'll never will. I miss her. I wish she was still here.

Love,
Bethann

Richard stared down at the letter through eyes filled with tears, and whispered thanks for a daughter so precious, and a second chance. Then he folded the letter, and tucked it safely away in his top drawer.

– Six –

*L*EAH STOOD UP to brush off her shirt and breeches, convinced she'd been resting a long time, and couldn't understand why she was still tired. Her hands were dirty, her boots scuffed and muddy. She couldn't find Shad. She couldn't find her home. And she couldn't find the horses. She knew she was right in the middle of the Maple Dale cross country course, yet she felt lost.

She sat back down and ran her hands over the moist grass, her fingers spread through the lush clover. The dampness felt tingly, inviting her to lie down, to nestle, to feel it all over. She raised her arms above her head and back down to her sides, again and again, then rolled over and brushed her lips against the dew. Her fingernails were anchored deeply into the soil, when suddenly her mood changed. She watched an ant make its way through the grass, carrying a fly three times its size. It climbed up and over and never once veered from its course. She envied it. It knew exactly where it was going. Exactly. It was going where it came from. Why an ant and not her? Why not her? She edged away from it and rolled onto her back, raised her fists to the sky, and cried out.

Bill paced back and forth between Christine and Walter's desks, pausing only to look out into the arena every so often at the idle equipment and shake his head, before starting up again. Walter was perched on the top bench of the bleachers, with his elbows on his knees and chin in his hands.

"Let's go for a walk," Christine suggested.

"What?" Bill looked at her like she was crazy. Walter did too.

"Come on, it'll do us some good," she said. "I haven't seen all of the northwest corner and now seems as good a time as any."

"I don't feel like walking," Walter grumbled.

Bill stopped only to nod in agreement before pacing on, but Christine persisted. "It's not as if we have other things to do. Besides, when this is all settled, we won't have time for these luxuries. Think about it. And I'll bet there's all sorts of qualities you could point out that I can use to help sell some of those lots." She was repeating what Walter had said to her just the other day, on purpose, and it worked.

"All right, let's do it." He jumped down off the bleachers and they both turned to Bill.

He shook his head. "I've seen it all."

"Not with us you haven't," Christine said, amazed by her own tenacity. "Come on. Humor us."

Why not? This standing around was getting to him. They all headed toward the door. "Who knows?" Christine said. "Maybe we'll see the cat."

Walter grabbed Bill by the arm when he turned on his heels, tugging him along, and the three of them were laughing as they started out. About a hundred yards or so up the trail though, they heard a noise. A howling sound, as if the wind had been given a mournful voice. And just as abruptly, their laughter ceased.

"What was that?" Christine gasped.

"Someone crying," was Walter's guess.

Bill said it sounded like a cat in heat.

It was anybody's guess. Whatever it was, managed to stop three adults of above average intelligence, dead in their tracks in broad daylight. When they heard it again, Christine backed up and took cover behind Bill, jokingly at first, but with her heart pounding in her ears.

"Jesus..." Walter chuckled to try to make light of it as well, but his pitch was too high and he sounded giddy instead. "I've never heard anything like that in my life. Have you?"

Bill shook his head and glanced over his shoulder at Christine, who was staring up at him wide-eyed. "No, but let's go see what it is," he said, already moving in that direction.

Walter's mouth dropped. "What? You want to *what*? You of all people with all your talk about strange?"

Bill laughed. "Strange ain't strange unless you see it's strange," he said. And with that, he changed his voice, imitating an old Cajun. "My momma tole me don't be messin' with them spirits, cause if they see you, they gonna get you."

Walter laughed. "So why do you want to go check it out then?"

"Because *that* I gets from my daddy. My ole man would check it out, yes sah! He would, uh huh, yes sah!"

"Oh? Your old man was brave, huh?" Walter said.

Bill shook his head. "No, jiss crazy."

Christine laughed now too, but funny as Bill's antics were, she was giving some thought to turning around and heading straight back to the arena. But then they heard the noise again and she decided she didn't want to be alone. Tagging along, she stayed so close to Bill she practically clipped his heels each time he stopped to look around and listen.

They walked on for some time without hearing it again though, and after a while, grew rather quiet themselves. The Maple Dale grounds were captivating, so captivating, that now whenever they spoke it was in praise of the hills of clover, and the apple orchards, and the peach trees, and the majestic hardwoods. Most of the trees had to be at least fifty years old, and stood proud, waving and fluttering their leafy fingers.

When they came upon a large willow, where beckoned an old park bench, they sat down to rest and were tucked in by large branching arms that responded gently to the slightest whim and breeze. Christine gazed out over the cross country course and in her mind, recalled Bethann's first show. Was she ready? Yes. Leah said she was. She remembered how nervous she and Richard were for her. She and Richard were still together then. Bethann was petrified.

"Take a deep breath," she could hear Leah telling her. "Take a deep breath. Keep your head. Make like you're doing it for practice. And go out there and do it right."

Bethann placed third that day to two seasoned veterans. As parents, she and Richard couldn't have been prouder. But their pride paled in comparison to Leah's reaction. "I knew you could to it," she told Bethann. "I knew it." And if she said it once, she must have said it again at least ten more times. "I knew it."

"What the hell?" Bill said, staring straight ahead.

Walter and Christine turned. "What?"

"There!" Bill pointed, then stood and walked across an area that had been cleared for a road. Walter and Christine followed, puzzled even more then when he stopped in front of a tiny tree, an oak seedling about two feet tall.

"This wasn't here yesterday," he said.

What? The tree? Walter frowned. "Maybe it was buried and just worked its way back up."

Bill glanced at him. "Yeah right. And when it popped up, it patted all that dirt down around itself too." He shook his head. "I don't believe this. Someone planted it."

No doubt about it. Even Christine agreed. But why? What on earth for? Bill bent down and touched it gently with his fingertips. "This is getting really weird."

Walter nodded and looked around. "Probably some conservation nut."

Bill counted the branches, eight, and all healthy. "Yeah, well whoever it is, has to know we can't leave it here."

"Maybe not," Walter said. "Maybe they don't know anything at all. You might as well yank it out."

Bill sighed, gazing at the little twig of a tree, then shook his head and stood up slowly. "I'll come back later and plant it over there." He motioned to a wooded area just beyond them and was looking for a good spot, when all of a sudden his expression changed. "What the...?"

Christine and Walter turned. "What now?"

"There!" Bill pointed. "The grass. What does that look like?"

It came to both Walter and Christine at the same time, but it was Christine who answered. "If this were winter and the ground was snow covered, I'd say it was a snow angel."

Bill nodded. That's exactly what he thought it looked like. "This is great," he said. "Just great. We got us a goofball roaming the woods around here planting trees and making snow angels in the grass. What next?"

"Klaus Bukener here to see you, Mr. Morrison."

Richard glanced at his watch. "Send him in." Klaus was nineteen minutes late, and worse, hadn't called to offer an apology or excuse. When they shook hands, Richard motioned to a chair.

"It's good you agreed to see me," Klaus said.

Richard nodded noncommittally.

"Nice office."

Richard nodded again. Christine had taken a lot of pride several years back in decorating it. She had exquisite taste, and had perceived a trend for muted pastels being declared masculine as well as feminine, long before it became vogue.

"Mind if I smoke?"

Richard motioned for him to go ahead, and while he lit up, took a good long look at him. He hadn't liked Klaus the first time they met, and lately, liked him even less. He was overweight and unkempt, and always gave the impression of having something more important to do. The stubby cigar that dangled from his mouth seemed a fitting summation.

The intercom buzzed. Richard pushed down on the broadcast button. "Yes?"

"Mr. Kirk is on line one. He's confirming his appointment for three today. Shall I set him back?"

Richard looked at his watch. "No, keep it as it is."

"All right, I wasn't sure," his secretary said. "What with the late start with Mr. Bukener."

"Three's fine," Richard said, staring at Klaus to make a point, and with that out of the way. "What can I do for you, Klaus?"

Richard had his own reasons for agreeing to see him, but wanted to know what was on Klaus's mind first.

"My father *wished* for a continuation of the equestrian program," Klaus said, puffing on the cigar. "He didn't demand it. He didn't stipulate it."

When Richard reached for his tape recorder to adjust the volume, Klaus paused, then continued, obviously annoyed. "So let's cut through all the malarkey. Are you for the project or against it? Because if you're for it, and I suspect you are, considering your wife's involvement, then we ought to be moving ahead."

Richard hesitated. "I don't believe we can do that. As you know, I haven't even read Leah Oliver's will yet."

"What? Jesus!" Klaus said, in an instant huff and spraying saliva down the front of his suit. "Three goddamned lawyers in on this thing, and no one knows what's going on! What the hell have you been doing?"

Richard's eyes hardened, but his voice was calm. "What I do with my time is no concern of yours."

"You're right. I'm sorry," Klaus said quickly. "But surely you're aware that all this legal lolly-gagging could very well ruin this project."

Richard smiled caustically. "Yes, I am. Which is the reason I agreed to meet with you today. It seems there's a document missing from Leah Oliver's personal possessions."

"So?"

"So..." Richard said, purposely looking distracted now while fidgeting with his pen. "Until we can locate it, her bequests can't be administered."

Klaus shifted his weight in another huff. "It wasn't her will."

"No, that's obvious, since Mr. Howell has it." Richard leaned forward, appearing to adjust the volume on his recorder again. He looked at Klaus. "You wouldn't happen to know where this document might be, would you?"

"Me?" Klaus's forehead started to shine with perspiration. "Why me?" he sputtered, launching a spray of spit balls across the top of Richard's desk. "Why are you asking me that?"

Richard reached for a tissue and wiped his desk, leaving Klaus with nothing to do but stew, and stew some more, until he finally looked up. "Without the document, Klaus," he said, "we can't move ahead."

"Why? What could be that goddamned important?"

"I don't know. Your guess is as good as mine." Richard glanced at his watch, then stood up and extended his hand. "But nevertheless, until we locate it, we're at a virtual standstill."

The more Bill and Christine and Walter talked about it, the more sense it made. What they were dealing with *was* probably just an eccentric conservationist, not unlike the ones who complained about the Century Home being destroyed. By the time they got back down to the arena, they were feeling pretty sure about it. At least it was a tangible explanation.

As they rounded the corner, Bill saw a cat dart into the barn. "Quick!" He motioned for Walter to go around back, he'd take the front. Christine was to watch to see if it came out. It didn't. And after a while of hearing, "Kitty, kitty, here kitty, kitty," in baritone and bass, she wanted to laugh. Here they were, the three of them, with seemingly nothing better to do than chase a cat. How ironic, compared to yesterday's hectic schedule.

Then everything fell quiet, the barn door opened, and there stood Bill and Walter. Empty-handed.

"What good are we?" Christine said, and burst out laughing. She couldn't help herself. And soon, Bill and Walter were laughing with her. When they'd finally run down and were all dabbing at their eyes, Bill looked back into the barn and sobered instantly.

"Okay..." he said. "Now explain that."

Christine turned to look. "What?"

"That!" Bill said, pointing to the blackboard.

Christine and Walter followed him inside. "It's the blacksmith's list," Christine said. "Why?"

> Persian Son - Thrown Shoe
> Plisky One - All Four
> Damsel - All Four
> Handsome Sam - Pads & Reset

Bill swallowed hard. "These names weren't here before."

Christine's face went blank. "What do you mean?"

"I mean, this board was empty. I cleaned it myself weeks ago."

"Then who...?"

Bill stared, just shaking his head. Good question.

Who?

A cold breeze swept through the barn, one that chilled Christine to the bone.

-Seven-

*K*LAUS COULDN'T IMAGINE which of Leah's papers was responsible for delaying the processing of her will, but rushed home in a frenzy to gather them up. He also couldn't imagine why his father had gone to such lengths to screw up his life, even after his death.

Actually, they'd never gotten along. Not like fathers and sons should. Why should now be any different? By all accounts, Klaus did care about his mother, but she died twenty years earlier from an inoperable brain tumor, taking with her the only real sense of family he'd ever had. His father never remarried, though Klaus knew for a fact that he always kept some whores comfortable and waiting in the cities he frequented on business. Because of this, Klaus had prepared himself for the surfacing of some bastard trying to lay claim to his father's holdings. It just never occurred to him, that of all people, Leah would be the one.

It wasn't quite dusk when he arrived at Maple Dale. His plan was to put the papers in a conspicuous spot in Leah's old office so that tomorrow he could show up, find them, and look surprised. He parked his car well past the barn and out of sight just in case, took the back way, and headed for the arena. A stiff breeze weaved through the trees around him with hushed sounds, whispering sounds, as the large sugar maple, singed from the burning of the Century Home, bowed sinisterly.

A wave of anxiety came over him, not unlike the others he'd been experiencing. He tried to shrug it off by walking bravely, marching actually. Double time. Hut two, hut two. When he reached the office door, he heard a noise behind him, and turned quickly. Nothing. It was the arena, its rafters creaking and moaning. Breathing. It sounded like breathing, inhaling and exhaling. In and out. In and out.

He couldn't stand it and tried to run, but his legs refused to move. He tried to scream, but had no voice. He screamed and screamed in silence. Panicking. He looked at his feet and then the ground. It seemed to be breathing too. Up and down. Up and down.

Off in the distance two lights appeared, growing larger and more intense with every passing second. A gust of wind knocked him against the building and almost off his feet. He let go of the bundle of documents to grab the door handle for balance, and gasped as the papers soared into the air.

Suddenly he could move again and ran to his car, with barely enough time to get down the other side of the hill before another car pulled up and parked next to the arena.

Richard turned the engine off and looked around. Christine thought she'd seen a car by the barn as they'd started up, but she'd obviously been mistaken. Probably just her imagination, she told herself, an excuse to leave. After all, when Bethann suggested they ride out and look for the cat again, it's not as if she really wanted to be a party to this. Not after today.

She'd tried earlier to tell Richard about all that had happened this morning, but Bethann was always present, and she ended up only telling them about the snow angel. Coming back at night was the last thing she wanted to do. But for Bethann's sake...

Bethann was out of the car first. She took one direction, Richard the other. Christine stayed in the car, listening to the radio as she kept watch, never once letting Bethann out of her sight. She cracked the window. "Bethann, you're going too far. Come on, it's dark."

Bethann waved.

"I mean it, come back." Christine could hear Richard off in the distance, calling out every name imaginable that rhymed with Phoenix. It made her laugh, and her mind wander. Then a gust of wind rocked the car, vibrating the antenna with an eerie sound, and she got the creeps. "Bethann, come on."

A piece of paper landed on the windshield, startling her, and she jumped. Another gust of wind, and it soared onto the lawn. "Get that!" she told Bethann.

Bethann chased after it. Her mom was a neat freak, no litter, no mess. An even stronger gust sent it sailing again. "Dad, g-g-get that!" she shouted. Richard grabbed it, and the two of them hurried back to the shelter of the car.

"Damn!" Richard said, shivering as he got behind the wheel. "That wind whipped up out of nowhere."

It's this place, Christine thought, and locked the doors. "Here." She took the paper from Richard to put in the refuse container taped under the dash, but there was something about the feel of it, the weight.

"Turn the light on," she said.

Richard flipped the switch and leaned toward her to take a look. It was the closest they'd been in over a year. They were almost touching. "What in the...?"

Bethann edged up to see also, draping her arms over their shoulders, and they all stared in disbelief. It was Leah Oliver's birth certificate.

Outside the car and not twenty feet away, another gust of howling wind scattered the rest of her papers. This, as the large sugar maple, unseasonably, released sap from its charred trunk.

Richard met with James Howell the following day. The birth certificate had been the missing document, the one needed to execute the provisions of the will. Leah wanted her parents found, and until an exhaustive effort was made, using the savings she'd set aside for the search, the distribution of the estate would have to wait.

Klaus hated waiting. He despised it! He damned Leah and he damned his father, incessantly, to whoever would listen, mostly his employees since they had no choice. But his reaction was mild compared to what it would have been had he discovered the exact reason for the delay. Leah wanted her parents found so that she could leave them something. Something precious if they cared. She wanted to leave them her memory.

In his own right, Klaus was every bit as successful as his father when it came to business, though their methods varied greatly. Klaus Bukener Sr. had a reputation for making shrewd moves by calculation and timing. His son on the other hand, leaned more toward preying on the weak and vulnerable.

Klaus always considered his father to be his fiercest competitor and arch rival, even now, after his death, and continuously believed this mess with Maple Dale had been done on purpose, a kind of checkmate from the grave. The old man's last hurrah.

"Yeah, well we'll see."

When Klaus was just twenty-three, barely dry behind the ears and fresh out of college, his father executed what Klaus considered the first move in this lifelong game they would play.

Klaus had made a costly error in judgment, one his father stood by, watched, and then chastised him for. Not privately, mind you, but in front of the entire board of directors. Embarrassed, Klaus accused his father of setting him up so he could purposely fall on his face. He ranted and raved, and threw a real tantrum then. No longer satisfied with attacking him as merely his father, he challenged his integrity as chairman of the board. This was something that could not, and would not, be tolerated. He had to be put in his place. Klaus Bukener Sr. would have the final say that day.

"My son's learned a bitter lesson here, even though he feels I've deserted him when he most needed me to bail him out. I apologize for this display you have just witnessed.

"Sit down," he told Klaus, as he himself rose to his feet and looked around. "But what my son doesn't know is that I *did* bail him out. I've assumed the loss personally." He shook his head sadly. "Yet here he is, thinking I've turned my back on him. My own flesh and blood. And all because I have allowed him to make his own mistakes."

He hesitated, glaring at Klaus. "Yes, I could've reached in and saved you, plucked you from the drowning waters you'd sunk in. I could've done that easily! Very easily! But you fail to remember that you didn't ask for my help. In fact! I'd say you went so far the other way, you forgot where you came from!" He pounded the table, oblivious now to anyone in the room but his son. "In business, Klaus, you don't get to the top by the seat of your pants. Nor do you get there with your daddy wiping your ass! It takes guts! It takes strength. And if you're a man, it takes even more than that. It takes a firm grip! Here!"

When the meeting adjourned, Klaus cowered out, and on the way to his office, made a promise to himself. No one, not even his father, under any circumstances, would ever doubt if he had balls again. Ever.

What little energy Leah had was slowly draining. Days blended into nights and weeks as she searched for the horses, and when she did find them, all she had to do was close her tired eyes and suddenly they were gone again. Her hunt breeches, which had always been spotless, were now stained and torn. And her field boots, once impeccably polished and pliable, had stiffened and faded, and were getting harder and harder to distinguish from the dirt.

The nights were colder now and often she woke to a frost that seemed to go right through her. She couldn't find a blanket and had to rely on what loose straw was left in the hayloft to keep her and Phoenix warm. Come morning, it was never enough.

The days kept her going. While the sun still defied the temperature, she roamed the grounds with Phoenix and soaked up all the warmth she could. When tired, she would settle down under a willow. They were the only trees that still had most of their leaves, the rest had fallen. One minute they were there, and the next they were gone. The willows were her only protection from the wind.

She leaned her head back against the trunk and closed her eyes. She could hear Phoenix stalking about, and could almost hear the thumping heart of a mole, hiding under the leaves, its fright sadly giving itself away. She knew Phoenix hunted from instinct, but wished he wouldn't torment his victims so. At the same time, she wondered how long it had been since she herself had eaten, and why she wasn't hungry.

She drifted off then and was in a dark forest. A forest in the shape of a tunnel, swirling round and round. She tried to grab the sides to keep from becoming dizzy, and focused on a strange light at the end of the tunnel. Sunlight, but in arcs, arms, stretching out to embrace her.

She opened her eyes quickly, only to shy from Phoenix as he feasted on his kill at her feet. She stared off in the distance, a minute, an hour, perhaps a day, then resumed her search for the horses. She was becoming impatient with them. It was Tuesday and they had to be rounded up for the lessons. Where were they? Where could they have gone? As she walked through the woods, everywhere, the time of year and neglect was taking its toll.

The grass was turning brown, the creeks narrowing. The paddocks and pastures, once clipped by grazing, were in need of brush-hogging. Weeds now choked the perimeters of the barn and arena. The clean smell of tanbark had been replaced with a musty odor. And mice, now rampant, ran across the beams and rafters fearlessly, all just two months from the day Leah had died.

Leah's parentage was readily obtained. Her father, Daniel Thorpe, was killed in the Korean War, apparently unaware of the seed planted in his fiancee'. Evelyn Ruminski was just seventeen when she gave birth to Leah, and only weeks after learning of Daniel's death. Poor and barely able to care for her ailing father, let alone a newborn child, she left the Catholic home for unwed mothers without looking back, less than twelve hours after she'd given birth. She denied herself the sanction of holding her daughter, a privilege she refused in penitence of her anger toward God and her country's army. She married at twenty-three to a John Collier, and at twenty-five, gave birth to another child, a daughter named Natasha.

At the time of the search, Evelyn had been dead sixteen months, preceded by her husband, who had passed away three years earlier. The Colliers had lived in Hudson, Ohio, and Natasha in Sandusky, where as a nun she taught school.

According to the information obtained, Evelyn left everything she owned to the Catholic home for unwed mothers, though there was no mention of the child she bore there. In Leah's file at the home, Evelyn had left a handwritten statement, composed only hours before giving Leah away. This, along with some notations made by the staff, was all the investigator needed to trace the rest. It's to be presumed that Evelyn's first born remained hidden in her past, but no one would ever know.

Richard laid the report down and looked across the room at Bethann and Christine, feeling as if he'd just read the epitaph of a lifelong friend. Leah's mother. How was it possible to have such compassion for someone you'd never met?

"Wh-what about N-N-Natasha?" Bethann asked.

Richard sighed and glanced at the report. "According to this, she's dead also." He hesitated. "It says she died on a mission for her faith."

"H-H-How?"

Richard read silently over the last paragraph again, and looked at Christine before answering. "She died out of the country."

Bethann got up and started across the room. "Does it s-s-say how?"

Richard nodded, but wouldn't let her see the report. There were too many details. "Apparently she died of malaria."

Bethann started to cry, and cried throughout the night. It didn't seem fair. Leah had never known her family. She never knew anything about them. And now they'd never know anything about her.

-Eight-

CHRISTINE FELT LIKE THE WEATHER, a steady, dreary downpour from a dull gray sky, that seemed to go on forever. Bethann had left for school a good half hour ago and although she was normally in the habit of leaving soon after, she couldn't quite convince herself to venture out. She'd made an effort, several in fact. She'd even put on her coat and opened the door, but that was as far as she got. She ended up sitting back down with another cup of coffee.

Richard mistook the slammed door as her leaving and came downstairs a few moments later, startling himself as well as Christine. "Sorry, I thought you left."

"I can't. I've tried. It's so gloomy out there."

Richard smiled as he sat down across from her, and was quiet for a moment. "Are you okay?"

Christine shrugged. "I will be," she said, implying she just needed to finish her coffee first.

Richerd nodded and got up for one himself. "I thought you cut back in the morning."

"Me? Why?" She frowned, and when Richard held up the almost full pot, realized what he meant. "Oh. No, I usually make another one just before I leave."

Richard looked at her. "For me? Thank you," he said, and no sooner said, he wished he hadn't. It was too late. The room filled with a sudden closeness, a penetrating familiarity, and Christine instinctively reached for her purse to leave. Shad was lying in her way, all stretched out, she remarked hastily about how trusting he was, how he never moved, and with that, stepped over him and started out the door.

Richard stopped her. "I love you, Christine," he said softly.

She wouldn't look at him. She couldn't. Not with the past welling up so vividly in her eyes. She stared at the door instead, an inanimate object. A second, maybe two. As long as it took to see clearly again. Then she walked out.

Christine, more than anyone, wished she could be different, wished things could be different. As it was, she could spend hours building a case for her and Richard's relationship, days. And at any given moment, one small thought would creep in and it would all come crashing down around her, scattering fragments of an eighteen-year marriage all to hell. If only she could be as forgiving as she was relentless, as bending as she was steadfast. But she was who she was, and if there was anything she was certain about, it was that.

While still in her teens, she knew exactly what she wanted out of life, and always, it revolved around Richard. They were going to go to college together, get married, have one or two children, live in a Colonial nestled by a brook on a brick-paved road in Chagrin Falls, surrounded by abundant wealth, and they were going to live happily ever after.

She planned to always drive a Cadillac, wear only natural fabrics, forgetting that such a thing as polyester ever existed, and her shoes would be all leather, not just the uppers. In the summer, she'd wear only canvas espadrilles, and only a neutral color. She would always be well groomed, never appearing to be anything less, would always wear the proper amount of makeup, minimal, a classic hairstyle and clear fingernail polish at all times. And her jeweled adornments would only be gold and diamonds.

Christine was one of three children. Her father worked as a builder's laborer, her mother a part-time secretary. They were a struggling family, financially. By the time Christine graduated from high school, she'd gone to nine different schools and had moved ten times. The one home she did love was an old farm house, where she entertained the idea of owning a horse. But her family relocated before she could save up enough money, and moved back into an apartment.

This aside, Christine was raised in an atmosphere of warmth and caring, chock-full of Sunday gatherings and family reunions. Her father was witty, smiled a lot, and had a hearty laugh. He loved to play pinochle, watch *The Three Stooges,* and was a man rich and abundant in family and friends. Her mother was very religious, was always praising the Lord when things went well and cursing the devil when things went wrong, and loved to cook. Their home was constantly filled with the aroma of things like fresh-perked coffee, homemade buns, pies, and pot roast. Christine's friends loved to tag along with her after school, knowing something fresh from the oven awaited them. Hot cross buns at Easter, gingerbread at Halloween.

Holidays were steeped in tradition. Memorial Day and the Fourth of July were spent picnicking at Metropolitan Park, the highlight being when her grandmother would swing a baseball bat at least once, to prove that she still could. Thanksgiving brought family for breakfast, lunch, *and* dinner. Christmas Eve her mother would spin angel hair on the tree to keep the magic safe throughout the year. They were permitted to open one gift then, new pajamas of course. Christmas morning always started with a prayer.

Even Labor Day had a ritual, the one responsible for it being Christine's least favorite holiday. It signaled the time to make the annual back-to-school trip to Zayres. In addition to the shopping cart being stuffed with three sets of loose-leaf folders, paper, spiral notebooks, pencils and pens, there were the clothes. Too brightly colored and too polyester as far as Christine was concerned. And a package of socks, nylons when they got older, one bra, a slip, and seven pairs of panties in assorted colors, with a different day of the week cheerfully embroidered on each.

Birthdays were grand affairs too. The gifts were usually home-made, wrapped in tissue paper, and secured with any kind of tape that happened to be around the house. But they were treasures nonetheless. She and her sisters always made gifts for her parents as well. And never once did they get the feeling that it wasn't exactly what had been wished for. Memories.

Then there was the family car. Old. Ancient. A clunker with mechanical problems. Appropriate terms for any car they had while Christine was growing up. Transportation specials that inevitably always broke down at the leanest of times. Often, as a result, her father had to walk to work, his huge black lunch pail tucked under one arm, an extra thermos under the other, and a bounce in his stride. A man who for the most part always seemed to be happy, though sometimes Christine couldn't understand why. To the best of her knowledge, he had never owned a new suit, even in his younger days, let alone a new car. Her mother too, was always doing without. Her wedding band had been bought at a dime store, the gold plating wore off after just a month or two. And her reading glasses came from the drugstore. Reading glasses and a magnifying glass.

This was hardly tragic by any standards, but on top of this were the conversations Christine overheard at night. The ones where her mother and father would talk about making ends meet. Arguments. Bitter arguments. Her mother crying, her father eventually apologizing. This was when he would always say, "Don't worry, we'll get by," word for word almost every time. "We always do, don't we."

Sometime around the age of sixteen, and after they'd just moved again, Christine began imagining a different life and the plan to have it. She saw no reason why a family with as much love as hers should *ever* have to settle for less. It wasn't that money was everything in life to her, it was just that it seemed to be the only thing missing. Yes, she told herself, I'm going to have it all. And while she was at it, she was going to make sure her parents had real wedding bands. And she was going to take her mother shopping. They weren't going to Zayres either. They were going to Joseph Hornes. First, second, and third floor. And not only that, she was going to park her brand new car at the end of the mall, so they could ceremoniously stroll past the five and dime. She even knew the first thing they were going to buy. China dishes. A set of twelve place settings to be used everyday, morning, noon, and night. And they were going to buy silverware. Not stainless steel, *silverware,* and enough so that it didn't have to be washed between the main meal and dessert on holidays.

Somehow she managed to do it all too, well ahead of schedule, and was comfortable in that happily ever after until a little over a year ago. Looking back on it now as she drove to Maple Dale, she wondered if she hadn't been so hell bent on fulfilling her dreams, that she pushed Richard into being an unwilling part of it, pushed him much too hard.

Richard on the other hand, grew up in an atmosphere similar to the one portrayed on the *Ozzie and Harriet* reruns. His parents were upper middle class, quite content in their neat little mortgage-free bungalow with black shutters that were painted every three years whether they needed it or not. Ideal parents. Parents who had their children's college money put away long before they were even out of grade school, longtime residents and pillars of the community. Richard's father was a patent attorney, and seemed always to be in a three-piece suit with a striped tie. His mother was a legal secretary when they met, but after marrying, retired to raise the children and never once missed her career. She had a full life with Richard and his twin sister Julie. And if she had any spare time, she volunteered it to her favorite charity.

Both Richard and his sister were the epitome of All American, looking very collegiate long before graduating high school. Perfect teeth, braces on at twelve, off at fifteen. And they were both quite athletic. Richard lettered in every sport he participated in, and his sister of course, was a cheerleader. They both served on the yearbook committee, wrote for the school paper, sat on the debate team, and never once had to pack their lunch because there was no money in the house.

Christine had been a cheerleader also, and she and Julie the best of friends, so it came as no surprise to anyone when she and Richard became friends, steady dates, and later, husband and wife. They were inseparable.

Richard idolized Christine and put her so high on a pedestal, that even he found her out of reach at times. She was so perfect, so sophisticated, she made him feel childish without even trying. When he asked her to marry him and she said yes, along with the excitement he felt, came a loss of breath, as if he'd just been kicked in the stomach. There was something about the look in her eyes that made him think he'd let her down someday, that he would never be able to live up to what she saw in him.

Evidently he'd been right. Though what had actually caused him, a man with seemingly everything, a loving, beautiful wife, an adoring daughter, a successful career and an iron-clad future, to chuck it all for a colorless liquid with a hypnotic acidic bite, would take years to realize.

Richard was not your typical alcoholic, at least that's what people who knew him thought, perhaps a bit confused with what typical was. He didn't drink from sunup to sundown, didn't drink everything he could get his hands on, he was particular in his taste, and never woke up in a strange place let alone a gutter or an alley. He was never abusive, offensive, or loud. And his appearance, gait, and manner when drunk, seemed to defy alcoholic gravity.

It just never really occurred to Richard not to drink. His father was a social drinker. He always had a highball or two to unwind from his day at the office, while his mother nursed a glass of white wine, and it seemed only natural to follow that trend. But the problem, the difference between him and his father, was there came a time when just one or two didn't satisfy Richard anymore. Faced with it later and told that alcoholism was an inherited disease, he felt sure when his ancestors handed it down, they bypassed his father, and dumped on him with a vengeance.

Richard never had blackouts, though actually at times he would have welcomed them. His memory was all too vivid. Not only did he remember the nights, he remembered the lies and alibis, and the trusting look in Christine's eyes each time he dished one out.

Then came that day, the day he broke her heart and shattered their lives forever. He'd awakened hung over as usual, with the events of the night still fresh in his mind. Christine had already gone to work and had left him a note of her day's schedule on the bedside table. Hard as he tried to focus, he couldn't make out a single word. He coughed all the way to bathroom, attempting to clear his throat of phlegm, and after almost gagging himself, looked in the mirror. A man he didn't recognize stared back at him. A man much older than he was and whose eyes were a different color. He shivered. This was the same way he'd greeted the day before, and the day before that. And the only thing that made things right, was the poison that put him there. He couldn't keep doing this. He just couldn't. He had to stop.

He turned and staggered to the closet, stared at all his suits, hanging neatly, and thought of lunch. Not that he was hungry. The thought of food nauseated him. He was thinking of the two or three drinks he'd have, and if he could only make it until then. He hadn't given thought to his client, his case, where they'd be meeting, or even the reason for the meeting. All he could think of was the gin and tonic.

Richard didn't go to the office that day, giving in to self-doubt and bordering on hysteria, he cried, until he couldn't cry anymore. Then he called Christine home, packed some clothes, and went out on the porch to wait for her, clutching his suitcase as he sat on the steps, shivering.

He will never forget the look in Christine's eyes as he bared his soul to her, confessing everything. Nor will he forget the endless tears that trickled down her face as she drove him to the hospital, or the way her hands were trembling as they walked down the corridor together.

A gray-haired woman peered over her glasses and offered them assistance. Richard had to clear his throat several times before he could speak. "My name is Richard Morrison," he said. "I need some help. I think I'm an alcoholic."

Physically, Richard was exhausted, and dozed off and on for hours after he was admitted. His symptoms of withdrawal were mild compared to most. But by evening, he wasn't sleepy anymore, and could think of nothing but the outpour he'd laid on Christine. And her silent acceptance. Routine tests were ordered, and the more he was wheeled from floor to floor, examined, prodded, and pricked, the more convinced he became. This was a mistake. He'd over reacted. He had obviously been under too much stress, enough to make him shaky, but certainly not enough to put him in a hospital. He didn't belong here. He wanted to go home. He had to patch up his marriage, and it couldn't wait.

He rang the buzzer for the nurse. If he could check himself in, he could just check himself out. But he needed his clothes. He would use this as a warning, and never push that hard again. He'd turn over a new leaf. He'd be faithful and never hurt Christine again.

That thought scared him. Because he couldn't figure out why he'd been unfaithful in the first place. Why would any man, with a wife as perfect and loving as Christine, be unfaithful? And what had made him turn to barroom pickups instead, women he never even cared to see a second time?

He rang the buzzer again. Where the hell was the nurse? He started pacing the floor, in a sweat, and was about to go screaming out into the hall for her, when in she came, with Matt Campbell right behind her.

"I want my clothes!" Richard shouted at them. "I want my clothes, and I want out of here!"

Matt looked him right in the eye. "No, Richard," he said sadly. "What you want is a drink."

Richard was discharged three and a half weeks later. His therapy had been intense, stripping him of any dignity he'd had left, with the family sessions being the hardest to sit through. Christine left each one feeling numb. And Bethann, frightened. For the first time in her life, she was seeing her father mad, angry. And her mother, withdrawn.

One morning, a little more than two weeks into his hospital stay, Richard faced what would be the beginning of his recuperation. He *was* an alcoholic. And he would *always* be an alcoholic. But as long as he never forgot that, or denied it again, he could fight the disease and win.

He returned home with Christine and Bethann, continued his therapy, and gradually resumed a full work schedule. Within weeks, at the office, it was as if he'd never been gone and nothing whatsoever had happened. While at home, and having settled into the guest room, absolutely nothing would ever be the same again.

-Nine-

KLAUS WAS RELENTLESS in his efforts to keep the Maple Dale development project moving ahead. He'd instigated action to invalidate the Coroner's report on Leah's death, citing the imprecise time as grounds. When that proved futile, he raised questions about the exact time of his father's passing. He threatened a scandal, insinuating the patients at the nursing home went hours between checks, even hinting at neglect. When no one seemed ruffled by those bullying tactics, he set out to try and invalidate his father's will on grounds of incompetence. But this too became an effort in futility. The will had been drawn up years earlier, at a time when his father's mental health was above reproach.

As a result of this obsession, he was spending a lot of time accomplishing nothing, to the point where he was beginning to lose touch with his other business holdings. He was determined to find a way. A loophole. He was positive there had to be one. And he wasn't going to stop until he found it.

Bethann was having trouble sleeping through the night and had begun to have a recurring nightmare. She would wake frightened, positive the dream had been the same, but within seconds, wouldn't be able to even remember who was in it, let alone what it was that had made it so frightening.

Bethann had always enjoyed school, her favorite subjects being English Literature and American History. She also liked Math, though not as much. She was a good student, but not the kind that didn't have to work hard. She loved sports and took great pride in her perfect attendance at all the football games. She and her best friends Stacy and Jessica went rain or shine. They even attended one in a blizzard, where they almost froze, huddled under the blanket her mom insisted they take. It snowed so hard they couldn't see the players and afterwards had to ask who won. But they were there. Most important. And they had a blast.

Stacy and Jessica didn't mind Bethann's stuttering. In fact, since as a rule she stuttered less around them, little attention was paid to it unless Bethann brought it up herself. Stacy thought it was definitely better than being flatter than a pancake, and Jessica thought it beat having acne, which was something she knew all about. The three of them were practically inseparable, roaming the halls together at school and almost always having a crush on the same boy, who generally never paid attention to any of them. Yet, despite this closeness, Bethann kept what was going on with Leah's will to herself.

Growing up almost overnight, it seemed, Bethann now took things much too seriously. She was determined to ensure Leah's memory be a part of Maple Dale, but didn't know how, and it was constantly on her mind.

In the midst of all of this though, there was something good happening as far as she was concerned. Something really good. Her mother and father seemed to be smiling more lately. She held her breath just thinking about it. And they seemed happier together. Not quite like before, but happy nonetheless.

Much to everyone's surprise, her mom had begun a ritual of early morning walks with Shad. She'd also given in to his pleas whenever she was about to leave the house, and now took him with her. She'd spread a blanket on the passenger seat of the Seville, since he shed so much, and always had to help him up and in, but he'd become her constant companion. She'd even take him with her to the grocery store, where he'd wait patiently in the car, dotting the lowered windows with nose marks, that he would then lick off, almost indignantly. And judging from the way he thumped his tail as they rode along, it appeared he'd even developed an appreciation for her classical music.

Bethann was waiting for them to return from their morning exercise, ready to go to Manchester for her riding lesson when the phone rang. It was Stacy.

"You'll never guess what Jessica heard."

"What?" Bethann said.

"It's so cool! She just called. She told me that her cousin Char, you remember Char?"

"Yes."

"Well, she told her that last night her and her boyfriend Randy were up at Maple Dale, you know, messing around, and said they saw someone. Like they lived there."

Silence...

"You there?"

"Y-Yes," Bethann said. "Who w-w-was it?"

"Who knows? They said it looked like a bag lady."

"A w-wh-what?"

"A bag lady! Can you believe it?" Stacy laughed. "A bag lady! Isn't that wild?"

Bethann shook her head and sighed, sounding distant and sad. "What else d-d-did she s-s-say?"

"Nothing, that was it. I guess a lot of kids are gonna go up tonight to see for themselves. I wish we could go."

Bethann didn't say anything.

"Anyway, I just wanted to tell you, with the way you used to ride up there and all." Stacy laughed again. "Can you imagine your riding instructor finding an old bag lady in one of her barns? Oh God!"

Bethann remained silent. Stacy had no way of knowing that she was still tied to Maple Dale and that none of this seemed funny to her. After all, it had been months since Leah died.

"Well, I gotta go," Stacy said. "I'll call you later."

Bethann hung up the phone and stared out the kitchen window, so preoccupied with her thoughts, she didn't even see her mother and Shad coming up the sidewalk.

Christine held the door for Shad and was sort of coaxing him along as Richard walked into the kitchen. He'd slept in after being up well past two working on some research he'd brought home, and was headed for the coffee pot.

"How was your walk?" he asked, patting Shad on the head. Christine's new routine was refreshing. He was glad to see her enjoying herself.

"Good!" Christine said, bending and stretching from side to side. "It was great! Shad stayed up most of the time. We only had to stop once for a rest."

Richard smiled.

"And believe me," Christine added. "When he sits down to rest, he sits down to rest."

Richard pictured it, Shad planted stubbornly with Christine tugging and tugging at his collar, and started to laugh. Christine laughed as well then, and neither noticed how distracted Bethann was, off in a world of her own.

Christine reached past her into the cupboard for the box of dog biscuits, low-cal treats for the mature dog. She tossed Shad one, he caught it, and she turned to Richard. "I think he really likes these. He had three last night and gulped them right down."

Richard smiled, about to tell her giving him that many was defeating the purpose, when all a sudden, Bethann spoke up. "There's a b-b-bag lady at M-M-Maple Dale."

"A what?" her parents said together.

"A b-b-bag lady." Bethann told them about Stacy's phone call and surprised herself by also telling them about how the kids were going to go back up there tonight. It seemed a little like squealing, but her loyalty was to Maple Dale.

Richard sipped his coffee, listening. "Maybe we'll ride up after your lesson and take a look. We need to take up some more cat food anyway."

Christine frowned. "Shouldn't we call the police?" She imagined a lice-ridden, gray-haired old lady up there, shotgun in hand and with her front teeth missing.

"Oh, I wouldn't worry," Richard teased. "I don't think the old girl's going to hurt us, at least not without a good fight."

Christine chuckled self-consciously.

"Besides," he said. "We don't want to get her in trouble, we just want her to leave. We'll just inform her that the landlord would kindly like her to vacate the premises." He winked at Bethann upon saying this, and got her to laugh too.

"You th-think she'll still b-b-be there?"

"Nah, she's probably long gone. The kids probably scared her off."

Richard parked between the barn and arena, swung the twenty-five pound bag of cat food onto his shoulder, and headed for the barn. Christine and Bethann took off in the opposite direction. Though months had passed, the air was still filled with the ominous odor of burnt wood. Foreboding, yet somewhat enticing, like the smell of burning leaves.

Richard put the food in the corner of the first stall, split it open, and started searching the barn. The tack room was empty, as was each stall, the feed room and the pump area, no signs of anyone having been there. He even checked the garbage cans. He climbed the ladder to the hayloft then. It was empty as well, aside from some chaff on the floor and a lot of pigeon mess and feathers. He hesitated looking up. There was something eerie about the open beams of a barn. It was as if he expected to see a body dangling from a rope. He raised his eyes slowly and let out a sigh of relief. Nothing. Not even a bat.

He walked over to the loft doors, opened them, and gazed out. From this vantage point, he could see practically the entire estate, even the lake up on the north end. It mesmerized him, the sheer vastness of it all, the shimmering... When he heard a noise behind him and turned, his heart skipped a beat.

The arena doors were stuck, so Christine and Bethann had to wait for Richard, and were just starting to get worried, when he came around the side of the barn. With a couple of good shoves, he had the door unjammed, and slid it open.

At first glance, Christine wasn't sure what bothered her most, seeing the jumps still in place or seeing all the equipment gone. Bethann, however, liked it just the way it was. She had a big smile on her face as she walked into the center and took a look around. She could imagine being on Persian Son, with Leah standing right where she was standing. She could see it all. She closed her eyes for a moment, and doing so, could almost hear the familiar sounds of horses, and laughter. And Leah's voice.

She glanced at her mother and father, standing in the doorway with the sun behind them. Their shadows were touching. It was like magic. Still smiling then, she turned and hopped over the first jump, headed toward the next, when all of a sudden she stopped dead and almost fell to her knees.

"Th-These jumps are d-d-different! They've b-b-been moved!"

Richard stared, suggesting, "Maybe they just got bumped." Christine nodded, agreeing with him. But another look around, and Bethann started to cry.

"No! Th-They've been m-m-m-moved They've b-b-been moved! This is L-L-Leah's beginner's course!"

Richard walked over and put a sensible arm around her. "Honey..."

Bethann pulled away, holding her hands out and shaking her head emphatically. "This is L-L-Leah's beginner's c-c-course! It is!" Tears streamed down her face. "Daddy, it is!"

Richard pulled her close, hugging her tightly as he looked at Christine, helpless to offer any explanation. And from less than a hundred yards away, Leah watched. She wondered if Bethann had fallen. She wondered why she was crying. And where was Persian Son? Had he run out of the arena? If he had, why wasn't someone going after him? And why wasn't Bethann wearing a hard hat?

Bethann wiped her eyes and tried to stop crying. Her father was telling her that there was probably a perfectly logical explanation to this. That maybe it was somebody's idea of a joke, albeit a bad one, but they'd get to the bottom of it. And she appeared to be listening. But then all of a sudden she gasped and pointed to the observation window. "Look! It's P-P-Phoenix!"

Richard and Christine turned just as the cat leapt into the air amidst a cloud of dust. Bethann ran to the window, jumping up and down to see where he'd gone. "Hurry!"

Richard fumbled with Christine's keys as he rushed outside the arena and around to the door. Christine, for her part, stared wide eyed with her mouth gaped, staring and staring. But Richard was too late. By the time he got the office open, Phoenix was gone without a trace.

Christine wanted to leave after this. "It's obvious the cat is *just fine*. Now let's go."

Richard had had enough himself, but Bethann wanted to keep looking. "In t-t-the barn. M-M-Maybe he r-r-ran in there."

Richard reluctantly agreed to take another look. "Fine, but then that's it." Bethann and Christine went with him. They got as far as the blackboard. Christine had eventually told them about the blacksmith's list and about what Bill had said, so it didn't really come as a surprise. Yet Bethann appeared shocked at the sight of it.

"What is it?" her mother asked.

Bethann pointed to one of the names. "This h-h-horse." She swallowed. "This h-h-horse is d-d-dead." It was Handsome Sam. "He d-d-died three y-years ago."

What was there to say now?

"Who's d-d-doing this, D-Daddy?"

Richard glanced around the barn, shaking his head, and ushered them out. He had to push hard on the door to secure the latch. As they walked to the car, a flock of pigeons swooped down on the barn, their wings fluttering and beating. While from atop the charred maple, a lone crow cawed.

Christine pulled a blanket off her bed and, wrapping up in it, walked over to the window. It was after midnight, well past her bedtime, yet she'd been tossing and turning for hours and wide awake. As she stood staring up at the stars, Bethann cracked open her door.

"Mom...?"

Christine turned and managed a smile. "What are you still doing up?"

"I c-c-couldn't sleep. I k-keep thinking about..."

Christine pressed her finger to her mouth. "Shhhh. Put it out of your mind." She motioned her over and wrapped the blanket around both of them. "Look. It's the Big Dipper."

Bethann nodded, and for a moment the two of them just gazed into the night. Christine thought about her own mother then. And how, if she were here with them now, she'd be insisting they pray about what was bothering them and wait for a Divine answer. Christine could remember praying a lot, without ever getting any answers, and had serious doubts as to whether or not anyone ever did.

"Can I s-s-sleep with y-you? I'm scared."

Christine hesitated. Her instincts told her to say yes. But then what about all those baby and child-rearing books she'd read, memorized practically, the ones unanimous in their opinion about not letting a child in bed with a parent? Soothe them and assure them that there's nothing to be afraid of, then take them back to their rooms. Be firm. Be consistent. Don't give in. You do it once, and...

"Mom?"

Christine nodded. "Sure. Come on." They both crawled into bed, tucked the covers up to the chins, and before long were sound asleep.

Richard had a restless night early on as well, and had just finally fallen into a deep sleep when he was awakened by a cold nose, warm breath, the sound of a thumping tail, and two big brown eyes in his face. He pulled his arm out from under his pillow and patted Shad on the head, hoping that would pacify him, and rolled over.

It didn't. Shad came around to the other side, sat down with a heavy sigh, and rooting his nose under the blanket, thumped his tail harder. Richard gave in. Considering Shad had made it all the way up the stairs just to let him know he had to go, how could he say no.

After their walk, Richard decided to ride out to Maple Dale and took Shad with him. He'd phoned the police last night after they came home and explained about the threat of possible vandalism. They said they'd patrol the area. But he thought he'd go check it out himself. Also, there was a part of him, a reluctant part, that wanted to take another look in the barn for that bag lady, especially considering what he'd seen, or hadn't seen in the hayloft. He stopped at an all-night convenience store for a cup of coffee, bought two beef jerkys for Shad, and started up the hill a little after five.

Leah stood facing the barn and didn't hear him approaching. Obscenities had been smeared across the white siding in bright red paint, and several of the windows had been broken. Furious, she raised her fists to the sky and cried out, sending vibrations weaving in and out of the trees, breaking branches, rippling the still lake waters and raising steam from frost-covered grass. For some time now she'd been confused. Confused, tired, and lost. Now she was angry. And with that anger, came strength.

Richard thought he saw someone by the barn and sped up the hill, spilling coffee all down his lap. Jamming the car into park at the top, which sent Shad sprawling to the floor, he got out, and took off at a run.

He circled around back, hoping to head whoever it was off and picked up a stout stick as he approached the corner. But no one was there. He darted his eyes across the field, turned quickly to see if the doors had been opened, saw that they hadn't, and threw the stick into the wind.

"Damn it!"

Shad had gotten out of the car by now, and was walking slowly up the hill wagging his tail, when for some reason, he stopped and started barking. Howling actually. The shrillness of the sound echoed through the empty trees.

Richard called to him several times, whistled, and had to clap his hands to finally get his attention. He came with his head low and his tail between his legs. "It's okay," Richard said, petting him and looking around, wondering what it was that had gotten him going. "It's okay." As the sun peeked over the horizon, profane graffiti greeted the morning.

Leah sat down and rested her weary shoulders against the trunk of a stately pine. She'd only just begun her task when she was frightened by the lights, yet she was all but exhausted. Phoenix was exhausted as well, and lay curled up on her lap as they watched

Richard hose off the side of the barn. When the sun rose higher, she gasped. Shad was lying on his side in the grass by the arena, and wasn't moving. He was just lying there. As if he were dead.

"Oh God, no..." She wanted a closer look, hoping it wasn't true, but couldn't face the possibility. Clutching Phoenix tightly, she fled into the woods. She was afraid of his death, she'd always dreaded it, and didn't stop until she was far enough away so she *couldn't* look back.

She tried telling herself that she was probably dreaming, and that Shad wasn't there at all, and suddenly started sinking into the ground. She edged back, wedging herself between the gnarled roots of an old oak, and breathed a sigh of relief when she felt somewhat secure. "Oh no!" She panicked again, and dangled poor Phoenix in front of her, wanting proof that *he* was still alive. He meowed indignantly, jumped out of her hands, and so typically feline, bolted, crouched down about ten feet away, where he twitched his tail and looked back at her. Then he quickly scaled a tree, and was gone.

By the time Richard hosed off all the paint, it was well past eight. Shad was still stretched out in the grass, sound asleep and chasing something in a dream. Richard nudged him gently to wake him and went into the barn to put the hose away. He searched the stalls again then, not once but twice, took another look in the hayloft, and decided he might as well go look for the cat. The food was being eaten, so he felt sure it had to be near. Shad followed along.

They came across a lot of squirrels and chipmunks, and a rabbit and then a deer, but no sign of the cat, and after a while turned back. Richard was getting hungry. About a hundred yards from the barn, Shad suddenly started barking again and took off through the woods. When Richard caught up to him, he was panting hard and staring anxiously up a tree, where curled up on a limb sat Phoenix.

"Well, I'll be damned." Richard glanced around, wondering how he was going to get to him, but needn't worry. The cat came down on its own, meowing up a storm, marched up to Shad whose tail was wagging furiously, and started rubbing up against him.

Richard smiled. He'd heard of cats and dogs getting along, but had never witnessed anything quite like this before. The cat was purring as he leaned down and picked it up.

Leah was getting impatient with the horses. She'd just found them again and was leading them back to the barn, when just like before, after she'd only glanced away a second, they were gone. First Shad lying there dead. Now the horses. And where was Phoenix? She called out for him, her voice careening through the brush. And at that instant, Phoenix turned on Richard, scratching, biting, and wrenching to get free.

Richard tried to hold on to him, but finally had to let go. The cat landed on all fours, disappeared into the woods in a flash, and left him cussing as he wrapped a handkerchief around his scratched and bloody hand.

Christine and Bethann were finishing their breakfast when he and Shad returned. "What happened?" Christine asked, reaching for his hand to see for herself.

Richard pulled away, then wished he hadn't, no matter how much it would've hurt. That was the first time Christine had touched him in so long. "It was the cat," he said, with a sigh. "I went out to Maple Dale to check on things and..."

Bethann got all excited. "You f-f-found Phoenix?"

"Yeah, but he got away. Sorry." Richard headed for the coffee pot and poured himself a cup. "He freaked out on me at the car."

Christine got up to add his cream and sugar for him as he told them what happened, and sat down across from him. "God, I hope it doesn't have rabies."

Oh great, Richard thought, that's all I need to hear. This grave-digging habit of hers used to drive him crazy when they were first married, always taking things one step further, always looking for the worst. "I'm sure it doesn't," he said, and sipped his coffee. "But just to be safe, we'll check its medical records. They came with Shad's."

Christine nodded.

"Oh, and by the way. There *were* some kids up there last night. They painted graffiti all over the outside of the barn and busted some of the windows."

"Did you call the police?"

"No, I just cleaned it up. It looks like whoever did it had second thoughts anyway."

"What do you mean?"

"It was smeared," Richard said, taking another sip of coffee. "As if they were trying to clean it off themselves."

Christine sighed, finding little comfort in that. "This is really getting out of hand."

Richard smiled. "The place is empty, Christine. Remember? It's to be expected. Kids do stupid things. Of course, not that you would know anything about that since you were never a kid."

Christine made a face at him. "Go ahead and make fun. But a crime is a crime, and this is getting weird."

Richard's smile widened as he just looked at her, and Bethann started to laugh.

"What's so funny?" they both turned asking.

"N-N-Nothing." She hadn't heard them talk like this is a long time, a very long time, and it was neat. "It's j-j-just..."

Richard ruffled her hair. He and Christine both knew what she meant. They even exchanged knowing smiles, though somewhat self-conscious ones. Then he stood up, saying how he was going to go unveil his hand and inspect the damages. The first aid supplies were in the upstairs bathroom.

A minute later he called for Christine, and fearing the worst from the way he'd said her name, "Christine!" she took the stairs two at a time.

She hesitated in the doorway. He was sitting on the edge of the tub, with absolutely no color in his face.

"It's..."

Christine walked over to take a look, and then just stood there. She didn't understand. "Richard?" She searched his eyes. "I thought you said you were cut."

Richard stared. "I *was* cut, Christine. And bleeding." But there wasn't a mark on him. "It was bleeding a lot."

Christine took the bloody handkerchief from him. It was moist and warm, it even smudged her fingertips. She sank to her knees at his side. "Richard...?"

He shook his head. He wished he could explain this, rationally, because it was what she wanted him to do. But he couldn't. "I'm sorry," he said. "But that cat scratched me. He scratched me several times, and he bit me."

Bethann appeared in the doorway. When they both looked up at her, she had tears in her eyes. There'd be no more denial.

Christine gripped Richard's hand. "Yesterday, Richard. At the arena." Her voice cracked. "When we saw the cat..."

Richard swallowed hard, nodding.

"Did the dust around it look like the shape of a person?"

Richard didn't answer. He didn't have to.

And neither did Bethann.

-Ten-

KLAUS FOUND HIS LOOPHOLE, and wasted no time implementing it to storm through the rhetoric. Maple Dale development was back in operation, with construction to begin immediately on his very own future home. And the lot he chose...?

"I'd like the one where the old Century Home stood."

He couldn't believe he hadn't thought of this earlier, not that he had any intention of moving there. It would be a cold day in hell. But who could prove otherwise?

He'd phoned Christine to list his present home on the market, and after that, phoned Walter, who in turn phoned Bill. Then he contacted John Smith, James Howell, and finally Richard. So much for their bureaucratic roadblocks. Things were underway. After all, Maple Dale had meant *so much* to his father. Why shouldn't he put down roots there?

Yes!

How much nicer it would be if Leah were alive though. He could gloat all the more then. Leah. He'd been thinking a lot about her since her death. Obsessive thoughts. He'd gotten to her in the end, and he couldn't get it out of his mind. She had become hysterical, so womanly, he could still see the look on her face. And he'd walked away from her, aroused, and feeling like a man. A man ten feet tall.

Leah roamed less and less as the autumn days grew shorter, and sank deeper and deeper. The grass no longer had a color of its own, taking on the hue of every fallen leaf now. Some fell straight to the ground. Some soared first. A final bow. Several bows. An encore. Then they too came to rest. A blanket of depression.

A red maple leaf landed in her path. A vibrant scarlet. She leaned down to pick it up, thinking perhaps it could soar one more time. It looked hopeful. But it crumbled in her hand, the wind whisking it off in hundreds of pieces, like ashes. Lost, weary, and desperate, she began to recite the Twenty Third Psalm.

"The Lord is my shepherd, I shall not want. He maketh me to lie down in green pastures..." The words were a comfort to her, so familiar. But as she approached the valley of the shadow of death, her mood changed. She raised her eyes to the sky, sure there was no such God watching over her, and lowered herself to the wet ground, as abandoned as the day she was born.

Bill and his generations of superstitious blood pulled up the hill behind Walter, and parked off to the side of the barn. "There's that damned cat!"

Walter turned. "Where?"

"There!" Bill pointed over his shoulder.

Walter squinted, finally saw it, and sighed. For the life of him, he couldn't understand, strange things considered, how Bill, all six-foot-five and two hundred and sixty-five pounds of him, could get so rattled by a straggly cat. "You're not going to start that again, are you?"

Bill mumbled something, and for a moment appeared as if he were giving thought to leaving. But then Richard pulled up, and soon they were greeting one another and shaking hands.

"Well, what do you think?" Walter asked enthusiastically.

Richard shrugged and glanced away. He doubted Klaus was on the level about building his home here, but had no legal recourse to stop him. "I don't know. I guess it beats having the place empty all the time. I was up here yesterday and had to hose off the side of barn. There was graffiti all over it. And those windows..."

Walter frowned, assessing the damage, but Bill wasn't listening. He was watching the cat, who was perched on a rock a safe distance away, licking his paws and watching *him*.

When Richard turned to see what he was staring at, his blood drained from his face. Dare he tell them what happened, even when he couldn't believe it himself? Hadn't he and Christine decided after being up half the night trying to comfort Bethann, to not say anything to anybody.

"I almost caught him yesterday," he found himself saying when the cat seemed to watching *him* now. "But he got away."

Bill looked at him warily, as if he knew there was more to the story, and that's all it took. Richard told them everything, cloud of dust, bloodless wounds, and all, as Leah watched.

She wondered what they were doing, what they were talking about. She recognized Richard immediately, but couldn't place the other two. She thought she'd seen them before, but couldn't be sure, like so many other things she wasn't sure of anymore. Not even her dreams. If in fact they were dreams, because she really couldn't remember sleeping anymore either.

They were far too old for riding lessons, and she was certain she didn't have a horse hardy enough for the large black man. They scared her. All of them. But especially the black man. He didn't belong here. And he was angry.

"I'm not afraid of anyone or anything that can stand and take a punch," Bill said emphatically. "But a cat that can scratch and bite without leaving a mark, is another story."

Walter started to say something, but Bill didn't particularly care to hear it. When he raised his hands, Leah fled into the woods.

"And he really caught me off guard too," Richard said. "He'd seemed pretty friendly until I got to the car."

"Well, then that's it," Walter said, trying desperately not to believe any of this. "It was the car. It scared him."

Richard glanced to where the cat had been sitting. It was gone now. He shook his head. "No, I hadn't even gotten in. It was the wind I think."

The three of them turned, and fell quiet as Christine's car started up the hill. Richard suggested she not bring Shad in lieu of what had happened yesterday. They'd also agreed they weren't going to discuss this with anyone. However, it was obvious to Christine from the looks on their faces as she parked and got out, that it was precisely what they were talking about.

"I told them," Richard said, confirming her suspicions.

Christine nodded, and as she looked from one to the other, tried to determine what each was thinking. "I know it sounds crazy, but the handkerchief, and the blood..."

Bill checked his watch. His crew and equipment were due to arrive any minute. He stared and looked aggravated. And Walter looked faint. Christine edged toward Richard. "Did you tell them about the other day too? You know, about the dust?"

Richard nodded, and for a moment, they all just looked at one another. Bill broke the silence. "I think what we have to decide on here, is exactly what we're dealing with."

Walter gulped. "What do you mean?"

"What do I mean...?" Bill *really* looked aggravated now. "What I mean is, is it vandals and a ghost? Or just a ghost?"

Walter started sputtering. "Oh now wait a minute! Let's not get carried away. Some odd things are happening, but..."

He was alone in his thinking, and Richard told him that, point blank. "Listen. I know it's a little hard to believe, but there's no two ways about it. We *are* dealing with a ghost."

Walter disagreed lamely. "It doesn't have to be. It could be something else."

"Hey, call it whatever makes you happy," Bill said. "But it's a ghost. I've felt one around here from the very first day."

"Oh Lord," Walter replied. "Come on, get real. I don't even think there are such things."

Bill let out a laugh. "No, but I suppose you don't have a problem thinking there's a heaven and a hell somewhere."

Walter glanced at Richard and Christine. "That's different," he said, shrugging.

"No, it's not," Bill said. "How you gonna get there?"

Silence.

"Right." That pretty much settled it as far as Bill was concerned. He crossed his arms. "Deny spirits and you deny the rest. Unless you happen to know someone who may have walked their way up or down."

"But..."

Bill shook his head and sighed. "Let me tell you," he said, and hesitated, not at all comfortable discussing this kind of thing. "When I was a kid, my grandfather came to see me. I don't know what he wanted, maybe just to say good-bye. But it was after he died."

Walter shifted his weight and glanced at Richard and Christine again before responding. "You were a kid, like you said. A child's imagination. Maybe it was just a dream."

"A dream, my ass," Bill said. "It was as real as you standing there denying what's staring you in the face."

"Um..." Christine cleared her throat, hoping to fend off an argument, if that's where this was headed. "You mean his ghost? Your grandfather's?"

Bill nodded. "He woke me up out of a sound sleep, standing by my bed, just looking at me." He shook his head, chuckling somewhat. "And I don't mind telling, it scared the hell out of me. I screamed I guess and my momma come running. She said I screamed like someone was trying to kill me."

"And did *she* see him?" Walter asked.

Bill ignored the implication. "No, he was gone by then. But she smelled his pipe tobacco. She thought I'd been smoking at first, but I told her what I'd seen and that I was sure it was Grandpa, and she never doubted it for a second. She told me I had nothing to be afraid of, that he never hurt me when he was alive, so I had nothing to fear from him now, so..."

When Walter started to object, saying, "But..." Bill lost his temper. "Damn it, Walter! You amaze me sometimes! What the hell's the matter with you? It happened! I've got no reason to be making this up! I saw him! He was there! And someone's here now, so start believing it!"

Walter cowered, not so much in response to Bill's anger, but from the depths of his convictions, and Christine had another question. "Okay, so what are we going to do?"

Bill looked at her and smiled, impressed by how calm she appeared. "You mean about the ghost? I don't know. I've never had to deal with one before. At least not one that stuck around."

Richard had to laugh at that, especially with the way Walter rolled his eyes. But the lightness at the moment was brief, because now Walter posed a question. "What do you think this ghost wants?"

"I don't know. I think the first thing we have to do is determine who this ghost is. My guess is that it's Leah Oliver."

Walter backed up. "Leah Oliver?"

Richard nodded, and Bill agreed. "I saw her up on the north end just before dusk one day. Off in the distance."

"So..." Walter said.

"It was before I heard she'd died."

"Okay, so what's your point?" Walter said. "She was here a lot then. She lived her, remember?"

"Yeah, I remember," Bill said. "And she also died here. That's what I mean. She was supposed to have been dead a week by then."

"What?"

Bill shrugged. "I never said anything because I wasn't sure it was her. In those riding outfits, everyone looks the same to me. Only now I am sure, because she had that damned cat with her."

Richard felt his skin crawl. When he had the cat yesterday, was Leah present then too? Lord. "We're going to have to try and keep this to ourselves. This gets out and..."

Walter nodded to himself. "We'd never sell a lot."

Richard looked at him. "Actually I was thinking about my daughter, and what affect this news would have on her."

Walter lowered his eyes sheepishly to the ground. He hadn't given anything or anyone else a thought. "I'm sorry. I uh..."

Richard waved it off, and just then, the first of a convoy of trucks, trailers, and tractors, started up the hill. They'd have to talk about this later. Christine suggested they meet at her and Richard's. Richard said he'd contact Klaus, since he thought he should be made aware of this also. And it was set for that evening.

Bethann calculated the last algebra problem on her test and laid her pencil down with a sigh. Her teacher looked up. He smiled, then buried his face back into the book he was reading, and she stared at him for a moment. Up until now, she probably couldn't have recalled what he looked like, and this, after practically a full quarter of classes. He was as insignificant as the color of the walls. They were blue. She had to look. No wonder. Her teacher was wearing blue as well.

She looked out the window and before long, sighed again. Her teacher didn't bother to look up this time, as if he knew it was her. And she wondered if she was as insignificant to him as he was to her, and would anyone care if he died?

Such was her mood that evening at home. "Why is it, MM-Mom, that n-no one seemed to c-c-care about Leah until after s-s-she died? Why didn't th-they care when she was alive?"

"You cared, honey. Don't worry about other people."

This seemed contradictory, but well intended, so Bethann let it go at that. As she went upstairs to do her homework, Richard came in the back door to the aroma of brownies.

"Delicious," he said, chewing one and reaching for another before he'd even taken his coat off. "Are we having a party?"

Christine smiled. Whenever she was nervous, she cooked. Whenever Richard was nervous, he joked around. "No, but I *have* been cooking all afternoon, so I hope you're hungry."

"I'm so hungry, I'm weak," Richard said. "Did you talk to Bethann about tonight?"

Christine walked over and started stirring something on the stove. She hadn't. "I tried, but..."

Richard sympathized with her. "Come on, we'll do it now." Shad meandered in then, and after Richard made a fuss over him, they called Bethann down and went into the den. They needn't have worried about Bethann though. She'd been the one all along trying to tell *them* that it was Leah.

"I stopped at the library," Christine said pensively, while reaching for several books stacked on the table. "And according to what I've read, a ghost, a spirit...can get confused. Misguided. Unsure of where to go. Leah's case is similar to one documented here, where a person died under tremendous emotional pressure, and just wouldn't leave."

"S-So what d-d-do we do?" Bethann said.

Christine turned to Richard, but he didn't have any answers either. "Maybe we'll come up with something tonight. Right now, let's eat."

Walter and Bill arrived shortly after dinner, and they all had to wait for Klaus. He would have been on time, but he'd been driving around the block wrestling with an anxiety attack. And even now, he could hardly sit still.

"Are you people crazy? A ghost?"

Walter encouraged him to calm down, he looked like he could burst a vein, and Richard recounted the circumstances leading up to their conclusion, leaving nothing out.

Klaus's face by now was beet-red. "Then let's get the ball rolling and make a lot of noise! Start on several homes, not just mine!"

Walter saw some merit in this. After all, it *was* Klaus's property, most of it at least. But Richard disagreed. He thumbed through one of the library books. "That might only make matters worse."

"Worse?" Klaus shook his head in a frenzy. "Then what do you suggest? Maybe take the deed down to the cemetery and hand it over to her!"

Richard drew a deep breath. "No, I'm just suggesting that we give this a little more thought."

Klaus sprang to his feet. "More thought? No! This is ridiculous! Do you really think I'm going to buy this ghost crap?"

Bill had been quiet up until then, and even now, didn't raise his voice much. "If you think this is a bunch of crap, that's okay. You're entitled to your opinion. But you're wasting your breath trying to convince us. You need to go out to Maple Dale and tell Leah Oliver how you feel. You need to convince her."

Leah walked aimlessly through the woods, holding Phoenix, and came upon a squirrel. It darted across her path, up a tree, and then over to the next one, chattering and twitching its tail. Amused by its actions, she tried to smile, but her face remained stiff. This inability to smile had happened to her before.

Frightened, she wrapped Phoenix tighter in her arms. He was cold, and his fur was rough. It didn't feel like him. This frightened her too. It had to be him. She dangled him before her eyes, a daily and complusive habit now.

"Oh, it is you. Thank God."

Phoenix wrenched free, and she lowered herself to the grass, being careful to hold onto the weeds so as not to sink into the ground. She inspected her boots. They had faded so, and were all but gone. She could hardly distinguish them anymore. Staring and staring and seeing only glimpses of one then the other, she suddenly smelled smoke and turned, almost burying herself, and gasped. The end of the arena was engulfed in flames.

"No...!" She raised her arms over her head frantically, flying, flying, and swooped down on it, drawing the blaze into her lungs, as distant sirens approached. Damning whoever started the fire, damning them again and again, over and over, with each singed breath, she defied it to destroy her precious Maple Dale. To destroy even one small part.

"Don't you dare!"

"Don't you dare!"

Though the sky was filled with smoke billowing high above the trees when the firemen arrived, as they flanked the area with their hoses charged and ready, a very puzzled, though very relieved fire chief called his dispatcher and declined a backup.

Klaus received a phone call shortly after that. "I hope you don't mind," he told Christine, when she handed him the phone. "I left this number with my service."

The discussion had come full circle, somewhat more civil now, and she was serving refreshments. "No, not at all."

"Yes," Klaus barked into the phone. "What is it?"

Christine couldn't help notice, no matter what the man did or said, how it always appeared and sounded rude. Even when he'd said, 'I hope you don't mind,' there was an distinct edge in his voice, like now.

"How nice," he said. "How?" And then, "How bad?" And, "When?"

By now, everyone in the room had turned and was listening. Klaus was pale as he hung up.

"Problem?" Richard asked.

"Yes, there's uh, been a fire."

"Where?"

"At Maple Dale. The arena."

Bill's eyes widened. "How bad?"

Klaus turned. "It's uh, it's out now."

"They say anything about the equipment?"

Klaus shook his head, staring off, and looked totally preoccupied. He was. He'd just realized his ears needed cleaned. He could feel them. They were dirty. They itched. "No, they didn't."

"Well shit!" Bill said, already up and headed for the door. Everyone quickly followed.

The far wall of the arena, from just below the main ceiling joist, was gone. Jagged, charred edges, were all that remained. Richard and Bill walked around assessing the damages, while Walter talked to the fire chief. Christine and Bethann stayed by the cars, shivering as they clung to one another.

"This could've been a disaster," Bill said, motioning to the tractors, which were enveloped in smoke but unharmed. "If just one of them had ignited..."

Richard nodded. "They'd have heard it in Timbuktu." The two of them stood there for a moment looking out the open end into the night. Tiny, glittering specks of light beamed down at them, as did the harvest moon.

Walter walked up behind them. "Kinda looks like a drive-in movie, doesn't it?"

It did. One so quiet and still, it was eerie. "Do you think she did this?" Richard asked.

The *she* he was referring to went without saying. "I don't know," Bill said, shaking his head.

"No." Walter was positive. "In fact, if Klaus wasn't with us tonight, I'd have sworn it was him. He'd be tickled to death to see it leveled."

Richard nodded, and glanced around. "Where is he anyway?"

He was just now starting up the hill, after having stopped at the corner store to buy a box of Q-tips. He pulled past the cars and over next to the barn to park, and just to be safe, cleaned his ears again. And then again, and again.

"I expected worse," he said, when he finally joined them.

"We're lucky it wasn't." Walter remarked, with a twinge of irony in his voice only Bill detected.

"What do you mean?"

Walter looked at him. "The fire chief said it snuffed itself out somehow. It was out before they got here."

This had them all just standing there, staring at the ruins for a moment, pondering how and why, when out of the corner on his eye, Bill caught a glimpse of Klaus pushing down on a bulge in the front of his pants.

Why, the sick son of a bitch, he thought. He couldn't believe it and looked away, shaking his head. Growing up where he had, he thought he'd seen just about everything. Obviously not.

"They say how it started?" Klaus asked.

Walter shook his head and shrugged. "Probably kids."

Probably. Which is why Richard decided to stick around for the night. Christine pleaded with him not to, Bethann was beside herself in tears, and during all this, Leah watched. From a distance. She wondered if one of them had set the fire. Maybe Klaus. He could've done it. Or maybe the black man.

Bill offered to stay with Richard, which helped him convince Christine to go on home. He sent her and Bethann on their way.

Klaus, thinking they *all* should go home, left in a huff, screeching his tires on the main road as he made the first turn and then again at the stop sign. When Walter left then, Bill walked over and got a crowbar and two flashlights out of his truck.

Richard smiled. Who in their right mind would mess with this man, crowbar or not? "Do you think the power'll be out?"

Bill shook his head. "It shouldn't be, there's no wiring up at that end."

The power was fine. They had lights, radio, and soon, hot coffee. All the comforts of home. Richard settled down at Christine's desk, and Bill at Walter's. After a while, Bill turned the lights off, the radio lower, and they both dozed.

Leah had been watching them for some time from the corner, and now edged closer. She was sure they were going to try to burn the arena down again, and was worried her lungs wouldn't be able to take on another fire. Her only hope was to prevent the onset.

She crept toward Bill. She couldn't allow him to wake rested, he would be too much for her then. She had to stop him now, in his sleep.

She crouched down next to him and listened to his breathing, remembering stories about how a cat could suck the life out of an infant by sitting on its chest. Inhaling and inhaling and inhaling. Only with each breath, it was she who felt suffocated. When she gasped, Bill woke with a start, and hit the lights.

It was the cat. It was staring down at him from the rafters, as innocently as a stuffed animal. It was going to be the death of him. "Get outta here. Go on."

Richard woke to the standoff, Bill staring up at the cat, the cat staring down at Bill, and shivered. "Ignore him. I don't think he wants anything to do with us either."

"Oh yeah, sure." Bill yawned and smiled, stretching his legs out as he turned off the lights again. "I just had the weirdest dream. It must be this place."

Richard sympathized. "Did it have a cat in it?"

Bill chuckled. "No. I was drowning, and someone was holding my head underwater."

Richard stared in the near dark, listening.

"The next thing I knew I was up on the side of the river and my momma was drying me off." Bill paused. "I haven't dreamt about her in years."

"You're right," Richard said. "It's this place. Nothing surprises me anymore, dreams included."

Bill chuckled again, and thinking more about it, laughed. When he was a kid, his momma used to tell him that he was going to meet the devil laughing, that it was his way. Maybe so.

They heard a noise then, both of them, and both reached for their flashlights. They heard it again. Voices. More than one and getting louder. Slurred voices. Bill crawled over below the arena window and eased up to take a look. Thanks to the open end and the moon, he could see fairly well. "It's kids," he whispered. "Three of them." And drunk.

Bill rose slowly, motioning for Richard to go out and around. The voices were right beneath them now. He waited and waited, let out a yell, and with one precise kick, popped the window out of its frame. It sailed over the boy's heads.

Richard hit the arena lights right about then, and Leah fled into the woods. The boys were screaming now, and she couldn't stand it. She looked back. The black man was looming over them and they were pleading for their lives.

"Oh my God!" She too begged for their lives. She knew this black man shouldn't have been there. These were just boys. "Oh my God!"

"On your knees!"

"Oh my God!"

"Now!"

The boys fell to their knees.

One started puking.

Hours later, and in the daylight, Leah ventured back, clutching Phoenix. Maple Dale was deserted, smelling of smoke, echoing cries.

She roamed the arena, wondering what had happened to the boys, wondering what had been done to them. "Please don't hurt us!" Their voices were everywhere. "Please don't hurt us!"

Then she saw for herself. Over by the window, and in a thousand pieces, were all that was left of them.

"Give me your driver's licenses," Richard had demanded. "Hand them over."

"But we told you, it wasn't *us* before! We just heard about the fire and came up to see it! We didn't *do nothin'!*"

It was obviously the truth too. And they were pathetic, what with the one puking and the others trying to keep him from lying in it. Still...

Leah gathered the torn fragments of their lives; pieces of their names, their addresses, their photographs, and cradled them in her hands, wanting to spare them any more pain. Then with tears in her eyes, she did the only thing she could. She buried them.

-Eleven-

RICHARD ARRIVED HOME with just enough time to shower, dress, and get to the office for his first appointment. Christine on the other hand, wasn't going anywhere, not for a while at least. She'd decided to keep Bethann home from school, since they were up half the night, and was going to make them a big breakfast. One that would warm their insides and make everything better. Bethann wasn't hungry though, and for that matter, neither was Christine.

"No bacon and eggs? No grits?"

Bethann shook her head. Even orange juice seemed a challenge. "Mom, do y-y-you ever th-think about d-d-dying?"

Christine put the eggs back in the refrigerator and sat down across from her. "Sometimes, I guess."

"Are y-y-you afraid?"

"Of dying?"

When Bethann nodded, Christine folded her napkin, trying to appear casual in answering. "Oh, I suppose a little. I think most everyone is to some extent."

"What d-d-do you th-think God l-l-looks like?"

Christine hesitated. She often wondered the same thing. "Like us, I guess."

"Like us?"

"Yes. You know, like it says in the Bible, that we were created in his image."

"But what if th-that means only h-h-how he sees himself?"

Christine didn't know how to respond to that.

"And how d-d-do we know wh-what we l-l-look like to him? Because if h-h-heaven's supposed to be in the s-s-sky and he's l-l-looking down on us, we w-w-won't look the same. We won't even b-b-begin to look th-the same."

Christine smiled sadly. If her mother were here, she'd have a ready answer right out of the scriptures.

"We probably l-l-look like ants!"

Christine chuckled.

"You d-d-don't really think th-there is a heaven, d-d-do you, Mom?"

Christine really wished her mother were here now. "There's a heaven, honey. I'm sure of it. It's where you came from."

Bethann rolled her eyes. "Oh, Mom..."

"It's true," Christine said. "And I'll tell you why I think so. When my grandmother died, I cried so hard, I didn't want to believe it. But my mother told me not to be sad, because she'd gone to a better place, and that I would see her again someday. I wanted to believe that, so I did. And I still do, only not quite the same way."

"How th-then?"

Christine shrugged. "I believe in things I see. That's what I believe in. And sometimes when I look at you, I see my grandmother. I see her in your eyes. And as long as I can do that, then she'll never ever really be dead."

"But w-w-what about the person who doesn't s-s-see anyone when they l-l-look at s-s-someone else? What if even wh-when they look in m-m-mirror they don't s-s-see *anyone* they know?"

Christine reached over and touched the side of her face. "You mean like Leah?"

Bethann nodded, her chin trembling. "Yes."

"I don't know."

By midday, Bill had had more than enough of looking over his shoulder. Paranoia was getting on his nerves. Not to mention his being reminded each time he looked at the arena, of a building from his childhood in New Orleans.

He'd just turned thirteen, a time in his life when one minute he could feel as old as twenty, and the next, nine or ten. It was Mardi Gras. And the building was a float barn, where black men would stand in line for hours, for five dollars a day pay and the privilege of carrying a torch in the parade. Only some never made it to the door, thanks to the heat of the day, the wine and the beer, the pushing and shoving, the broken bottles, and the blood. Bright red blood to entertain the white people who were leaning over their banisters, watching from the housing project across the street.

Nigger watchers, Bill called them, laughing with his friends. "Friggin nigger watchers."

Then this one day it was his older brother who got stabbed, and who came staggering down the street toward him with blood spilling everywhere. His blood, his sister's blood, his mother's and father's blood. Bill bled as well, inside, and that night, thirteen-years old and with tears in his eyes, set fire to the float barn.

"Nigger watchers! Friggin nigger watchers!"

Nothing changed though. He shook his head, staring at the arena. How naive he was to have thought it would. The following year, the black men were lined up outside a new float barn putting on another show, and his brother was right back there with them.

Klaus pulled up next to the arena, nodded as he walked past Bill, and went inside to see Walter, who greeted him cheerfully.

"Good afternoon!"

Klaus grumbled. "What's so good about it?"

Nothing, Walter thought, now that you're here. "What can I do for you?"

"A lot," Klaus said, making himself comfortable on Christine's desk. "But for starters..."

Walter's mind wandered. It was the same old stuff, moving ahead faster, getting things going, and all that. As if he wouldn't if he could. "Can't you do some clearing? What about the roads? Wells? Sewer?" On and on and on.

A cool breeze swept through the office, and Walter turned, thinking someone had opened the door.

No one was there.

"What are you looking at?" Klaus asked impatiently.

"Nothing," Walter said, sniffing. "Do you smell something?" The breeze was spicy, like cinnamon.

Klaus shook his head, but he was lying. He knew the scent. It was Leah's. He knew it better than anyone. "No."

"You sure?" Walter asked.

Klaus didn't reply, his eyes suddenly getting bigger and bigger as he stared at a bird in the arena, fluttering against the remaining pane of glass. Walter turned, saw it as well then, and waved his arms up and down to scare it off.

It fluttered still.

"Get!"

It banged its head.

"Get!"

It banged its head again and again. And again and again, dotting the window with specks of blood.

"Get!"

The bird fell to the ground and Walter went over to take a look. Its wings were battered. Its sides heaving.

"The stupid thing," he said, glancing over his shoulder at Klaus. "Why didn't it just fly away?"

Klaus was on his feet and leaving. "Why are you asking me? How should I know?"

Bill came into the arena to see what all the commotion was about. "Oh Jesus," he said under his breath. Birds meant death, and there was blood everywhere.

Christine and Bethann pulled up outside. Bill recognized the sound of the Seville's diesel engine, and hurried out to head them off.

"What are *you* doing here?" he asked.

Christine was a little taken aback. All right, so she wasn't supposed to come in today. So?

"And shouldn't you be in school?" he said to Bethann.

"We came to look for the cat." Christine answered for both of them. "We think Leah might be worried about it, and we..."

Bill shook his head, appearing not the least bit interested, and Christine started past him toward the office, herding Bethann with her.

Bill blocked their way. "I saw him up on the trail," he said, pointing behind them. "That one there."

Christine backed up and nodded, nudging Bethann in that direction. Once they were out of sight, Bill went in and got some paper towels to clean the window, and disposed of the bird.

That evening, Christine told Richard about the way Bill had behaved. "I mean, he was really rude." They hadn't found the cat either. "It was like..."

Richard looked at Bethann. She shrugged. And because of that shrug, he defended Bill and changed the subject. "The man didn't get a whole lot of sleep last night, Christine. Don't take it personally. Besides, I've been thinking about something all day, and I need to talk to you two about it."

He had a theory on why Leah Oliver was refusing to leave. He'd even talked to Matt Campbell about it. "It's the cat."

"The cat?"

This was nothing new. "I know. But it makes more sense now. Her obsessiveness, the way she had the will written and everything, wanting each detail carried out to the letter. I think the cat being there is what's got her confused."

"Ph-Ph-Phoenix," Bethann said.

Richard looked puzzled at her.

"His n-n-name is Phoenix."

Richard smiled. "Okay, Phoenix."

Shad perked his ears, and Christine reached down and patted his head. "But what about her obsession with Maple Dale? What about it being the reason?"

"Matt and I talked about that too."

"What did he say?"

Matt was a firm believer in the supernatural, which would seem odd to most people, his being a psychiatrist. "He thinks it could be both, but agrees, that it could be just the cat."

"Ph-Phoenix," Bethann corrected again.

Richard grinned. He'd called Phoenix *the cat* on purpose that time, just to get her. She was as persnickety as her mother. "How do you spell it?" he asked, as if that would help him remember next time.

Bethann giggled. "Dad."

Times like these, even Christine felt like they were almost a real family again. "What else did Matt say?"

Richard shrugged. "Oh, a lot of *psyche'* this, and realms of that, and planes and avenues."

"He's not suggesting we have a seance of anything like that, is he?"

Richard laughed. "No. No seances."

Bethann had an even more difficult time sleeping that night, and woke repeatedly from a different dream now, played over and over. She was floating, soaring toward Maple Dale above the streets and following the same path she'd take if she were in a car. Stoplights, turns, faster and slower for traffic. Frightened. Frightening. People reaching up to get her down always just missed her, a paper boy came close, she felt him graze her foot. Then she was at Maple Dale, trying to stop, and sailed right over it. Every time. Over and over. She could get there, but she couldn't stop.

In the morning, she heard Matt Campbell talking to her mother and father in the kitchen, and came down to join them. Matt was jogging in place at the back door. "Good morning!"

Bethann smiled sleepily.

"I was just telling your mom and dad about my being up all night thinking about this Leah Oliver."

Matt never rested, and they all knew that, so no one apologized for his not getting any sleep. He thrived on it.

"And I think..." He checked his pulse and adjusted his pace accordingly. "I think in her confusion, she may not be able to separate Maple Dale from the cat, or the cat from Maple Dale. They may be one and the same to her. Who knows? But regardless, you're going to have to figure out a way to get her to leave."

"Wh-Why?" Bethann's mouth dropped. "Why c-c-can't we just let h-h-her be?"

Matt stopped jogging and with a sigh, walked over and took hold of her hands. "Because you can't, Bethann. Your friend is lost. You have to understand that."

But she didn't. Not at all.

"She's in limbo, and that's nowhere. In fact, it's probably worse than being lost. You have to help her."

Tears welled up in Bethann's eyes and Christine started across the kitchen toward her, but Richard touched her arm, shaking his head.

"But I d-d-don't know what to do. I don't know h-h-how to h-h-help her."

Matt searched Bethann's eyes, the tears streaming down her face. "You must. You cared for her the most."

Shad rose slowly from beneath the table to root his nose under Bethann's hand, and seemed to do it so instinctively to comfort her, Christine had to look away. She wondered how many times he'd done the same thing when Leah was crying.

"You have to think of a way to reassure her, to let her know it's okay to go. Think of how she was, think of what meant the most to her, and figure out a way."

Bethann nodded, gazing down at Shad and petting him, and Matt smiled reassuringly. "Use your heart, Bethann. Use your heart. And remember, I'm only a phone call away."

When Bethann nodded again, Matt resumed jogging. Richard followed him outside.

"What do you think? Is she okay?"

"Relatively."

Richard stared off. "I don't know what to do. I honestly don't."

Matt stopped exercising to get a good look at Richard's eyes. "What about you? You okay?"

Richard nodded. He meant about drinking. "Not even tempted."

"Good," Matt said, pacing himself again. "Good, because there's something else."

Richard drew an apprehensive breath, watching Matt jog up and down.

"The timing."

"What timing?"

"Halloween."

Richard swallowed. It was tomorrow.

"Strange things happen around now, unexplained things."

"What are you saying?"

"I don't know. I just know that Leah Oliver's not where she's supposed to be. Particularly now."

Bill had also had a restless night, and first thing upon arriving at Maple Dale, started on the arena. He could handle the open wall, just not the charred, jagged edges.

Leah watched him. The arsonist. The man responsible for those three boy's lives. A black man.

If only he hadn't come here. If only he'd stayed where he belonged.

She crept closer.

If only...

Bill stacked all the wood in a pile and gathered some twigs and dried leaves.

If only...

When he bent down and lit a match, Leah gasped. She had to stop him, before he burned all of Maple Dale down. She had to. She raised her arms, praying for strength as she crept closer, closer and closer. And just then Bill stood up, and she found herself inside of him.

His heart stopped. He'd heard something, a hissing sound, the sound a cat makes. He felt something too. Something cold. "Leah? Leah Oliver? Is that you?"

"Oh dear God!" She was trapped. She couldn't get out. "Dear God!"

Bill stepped back and turned, saying, "Don't be afraid. Please don't be afraid." He tried desperately to reassure her. But suddenly, finding herself on the outside again, Leah panicked and fled into the woods.

-Twelve-

CHRISTINE AND BETHANN spent well over three hours in the afternoon searching again for Phoenix, but he was nowhere to be found. None of Bill's men had seen him either, and for some reason, the fact that they had even inquired about him seemed to irritate Bill. Christine could tell.

Bethann however, hadn't picked up on it, and solicited his help. "I m-m-made a sign." She motioned to the car and he followed her. "But I d-d-don't know where t-t-to put it."

Bill just stood there when she took it out of the back seat. It read:

> *Leah,*
>
> *Shad and I are fine.*
> *Phoenix is being fed well.*
> *He likes being free. But*
> *I will always take care of*
> *him. Don't worry.*
>
> > *Love,*
> > *Bethann*

Christine held her breath, praying that just once, just this once, Bill wouldn't be so gruff, that he would say something nice. This wasn't easy for Bethann. But he just shook his head.

"What d-d-do you think?" Bethann asked. "Think it'll ww-work?"

Bill took a second or two in answering, and had to clear his throat to speak. "It can't hurt, I guess."

Bethann smiled. "Where c-c-can we put it?"

Again, Bill hesitated. He didn't want to chance his men coming across it. "I don't know. What about the hayloft?"

Perfect, Bethann thought, and Christine tagged along after them. She was deathly afraid of heights, but wasn't about to allow Bethann up the ladder and out of sight with Bill alone.

Bill placed the sign in a spot he and Bethann found agreeable, and Bethann felt hopeful. It was the only thing she could think to do. Christine tried to assure her on the way home. "Maybe it'll work, honey. Who knows?"

Bethann nodded.

"And don't let Bill's attitude bother you. He's always like that."

Bethann looked puzzled.

"You know. Mean."

"I don't th-think he's m-m-mean."

Christine glanced at her, then shrugged. "Maybe not. But I have to admit he scares me."

"Why?"

"I don't know. He just does."

"But aren't you g-g-glad he's g-g-going to be with D-Dad again tonight?"

Of course she was. "That's different."

"H-How?"

Christine kept her eyes on the road. "I don't know." Why did he frighten her? "Maybe it's just his size."

Or maybe perhaps it was because he was black.

"I'm just not comfortable around him."

Richard and Bill were once again guarding Maple Dale, and in for a night.

"Gin!"

It was ten o'clock on a yet uneventful Halloween.

"I give up!" Richard threw his cards on the table. "You obviously gambled for a living at some point in your life."

Bill laughed. "Hey, some of us are just lucky and some of us aren't."

Richard shook his head, smiling, and stood up and stretched. They'd been playing cards for over an hour, and he hadn't won a single hand. "I've never been lucky at anything."

Bill leaned back in his chair and crossed his arms. "That doesn't say a whole hell of a lot for Christine, you know."

Richard chuckled. "Oh, but it does. See, that was bad luck on her part."

Bill laughed.

A friendship was developing, one that could only happen sometimes by chance.

"I mean, talk about getting dealt a bad hand."

Bill's expression grew serious. "Awe come on, don't be so hard on yourself. Nobody's perfect, you know."

Richard raised an eyebrow, and the two of them laughed. After all, this was Christine they were talking about. A woman as flawless as they came. "You have *no idea.*"

A shiny red van pulled off the road and backed in behind a clump of trees to the one side of the Maple Dale entrance. Its occupants, four college freshmen couples, were filled with anticipation as they passed around a bottle of peach schnapps. This Halloween was going to be a memorable one for them. More memorable than their ghoulish costumes, and even more memorable than all their fondling.

There was a witch and a warlock, who'd done it all before, and a devil and a temptress, who barely knew each other's names, a Frankenstein and his bride, who were fighting but about to make up, and a Dracula, who was telling lies to his chalky draculette, as she sat on his lap, rocking slowly back and forth.

They'd come to Maple Dale from a boring party looking for some thrills, only with it lit up like a Christmas tree, they'd taken to thrilling each other right where they were.

Richard thought he heard something, and as he and Bill stopped talking a moment to listen, Leah watched curiously from the corner.

"Must be my imagination," Richard said, when he didn't hear it again.

"Let's hope so."

Richard smiled. "What do you make of Halloween, really? You know, all the talk about spirits and stuff."

"You mean, do I believe it?"

Richard nodded.

"Yeah, I believe it." He believed it all. "All except for the bull-shit," he said, which he didn't bother to distinguish. And that led to stories from when they were kids, and where they each grew up.

"Swimming in the river."

"The suburbs."

"In trouble once."

"Me...never."

"Had it made, huh?"

Richard nodded. "Yeah, I found trouble later."

Bill studied him, a silver-spoon-in-the-mouth white boy if he'd ever seen one, and yet. "Where was it at?"

Richard hesitated. "At the bottom of a bottle."

Bill swallowed hard. His father was a drunk. Richard and he didn't look anything alike. "How'd you quit?"

Richard was silent for a moment, thinking about Christine driving him to the hospital that day, and Bethann when she came to see him. "The hard way I guess."

Bill smiled. "Shit! You mean there's an easy way?"

Richard laughed, and then they both kind of sighed. It was getting close to midnight.

"What about Christine?"

"You mean growing up?"

Bill nodded. "She have it made too?"

Richard shook his head. "No."

Bill stared at him. He'd expected to hear how she'd been even better off than him, and how he had to beg for her family's permission to marry her.

Not so. "But she takes nothing from anybody," Richard said proudly. "I mean, nothing."

Bill smiled, *that* he knew, and wondered now about Leah Oliver, how she'd grown up. She too had appeared as uppity as they came, always in that riding outfit and scowling at him. That hunt-club scowl. Richard told him otherwise.

"She was an orphan. Didn't you know?"

Bill shook his head, and they grew quiet, unaware of the cloud of dust that had stirred in the corner behind them.

"Well," Richard said after a moment. "I guess if anything's going to happen, it'll be soon."

Bill glanced at his watch, nodded, and stared out into the arena. Richard got up and poured them both a cup of coffee. "Did you ever hear anything about the uh..." He hesitated. What should he call them? "Spirits of the evil departed, coming to claim the lost ones? The ones in limbo."

Bill nodded. Yes, he'd heard about it, and he'd heard it was true. He'd heard it from his momma. "I think if Leah Oliver's hanging around, she'd better find a place to hide."

Leah gasped! It sounded like a shrieking cat. And sure enough, when Richard and Bill turned, there was Phoenix jumping from one rafter to another.

"Oh Jesus!"

A second later, he was with Leah out in the night. Hiding. She had to get into hiding. But where? She darted her eyes frantically, and fled, but her legs blended into the darkness and she couldn't see where she was going for watching where she'd been. Then she fell backwards, and found herself in a hole.

Klaus's excavated basement. It crowded her from all sides. Phoenix was nowhere, and a hand started smothering her. A hand larger than her face. Then many hands, and voices. Voices moaning and crying out.

"Come with us... Come with us now..."

"No! Get away from me!" She could see the voices. She couldn't hear them, she could see them. It was all she could see. They were as dark as the night and touching her. Touching her all over.

Some were riding horses. Horses with no heads, whose jugular veins pumped blood in spurts. And some dangled cats, cats as big as dogs who'd lost all color and whose lifeless limbs swayed back and forth like pendulums.

"Get away from me!"

"Come with us..."

Leah tried to run from them, but the darkness overwhelmed her, and she kept bumping into walls. "Leave me alone!"

"Help us! Help us!"

"I can't! Get away from me!"

They pawed at her, groping and tearing. The voices, the voices of death, and she fell deeper, deeper, and deeper, fighting them. And then everything went blank.

Richard and Bill were talking and since the cat had left, hadn't heard a thing. "So even if I can get Klaus to agree to split the property and allow Bethann her third to remain undeveloped, the third we'd want would be the one he'd fight the hardest for."

Bill crossed his arms, agreeing, and *now* they heard something. Voices. Distant voices, coming up the hill.

Having been through this once, they moved swiftly into action. Richard hurried out and around to the side entrance of the arena while Bill poised himself to the right of the open window, ready to jump, when all of a sudden a bolt of lightning ripped through the sky, rendering the arena to complete darkness. They hear screaming.

"Oh Lord!" Bill gasped.

Then came the rain, pounding the roof and sounding like a stampede.

"Richard?"

"Yeah!"

The screams coming up the hill grew shriller as Leah opened her eyes to the pelting rain. The voices were still around her. She couldn't see them, she could only hear them now.

And laughter.

Lightning lit the sky again, enabling her to see her way out, and she fled to where she thought Phoenix might be. The office.

Bill's heart jumped when he heard a noise behind him. It was the cat, it had to be, that same scratching noise overhead. That same closeness. But the voices were growing closer now too.

Leah hovered behind him, whispering. "Don't let them get me. Please don't let them get me."

"Richard!"

"Yeah!"

The voices grew in force.

Bill didn't know which way to turn.

Leah hovered closer. "Please... They're coming."

A bolt of lightning showed their faces. The witch and the warlock, Dracula and his blood-thirsty draculette. Frankenstein and his wife and the temptress. And leading the way, the devil himself.

"What the hell?!" Bill's voice filled the arena.

It was the kids from the van, wet, dripping, and covered with mud. They'd heard screaming, they said, screaming like you couldn't imagine. "It even rocked the van!"

So *they* started screaming.

"Then we got stuck!"

"We tried to push it out, that's how we got muddy!"

"But it's buried."

"Buried to the axle."

An hour later, after two of the young men's parents had arrived to take them home, Richard and Bill watched the tow truck pull the van out. It had stopped raining, the lights were back on, and everything was calm once again.

They doubted if any of the parents would believe the story about voices rocking the van. They doubted they'd be listening to much of anything the kids had to say. It was too bizarre to be the truth.

"Do you think they'll be back?" Richard asked, making himself comfortable again at Christine's desk.

Bill laughed. "No, I don't think so."

Neither did Richard. He was quiet for a moment. "What do you think they heard? Really, I mean."

Bill shook his head, and then shrugged. They both dozed shortly after that, and it was Bill who woke first. "Oh my God..." he whispered. "Richard! Richard, wake up!"

When Richard opened his eyes, Bill motioned for him to look out into the arena.

It was Leah. It was her.

She was arranging jumps for the day's lessons. The class had been doing so well, she felt it was time to challenge them further, and was making the course more difficult.

Somewhat darker than life's air, transparent and yet visible, like the shimmering heat on a hot summer day, she moved gracefully, precisely, and took her time. When she was done, she stepped back to survey her work, satisfied, then went to look for the horses. And as Richard and Bill watched in amazement, she vanished right before their eyes.

-Thirteen-

BETHANN WAS AWAKE most of the night, dozing only to float over everyone she knew, again and again, and thanked God for morning. She wanted to go to Maple Dale, and suggested she and her mother take her dad and Bill breakfast. Pancakes and sausage from McDonald's. To their surprise, Matt Campbell drove up the hill right behind them.

"You know me," he said cheerfully as he got out. "Fingers on the pulse and all that."

Christine smiled. Where would they be without Matt? "If I'd known you were going to be here."

"No thanks." He wouldn't have wanted anything to eat anyway, not unless it was herbs, grains, and something freshly squeezed. Once inside, he took one look at what they'd brought, and bemoaned on behalf of Richard and Bill's arteries and pancreases. "That stuff'll kill you for sure!"

"So will starving," Bill said, smiling as he added lots of syrup. Richard introduced them, and soon they were recounting the night.

"Well, that does it then," Matt said, stepping up and down on the bleacher. Up and down. Up and down. "Something's got to be done."

Bethann stared into the arena.

"Because as long as she keeps existing as if she's..."

Bethann sighed. "I still d-d-don't see why we c-c-can't just l-leave her alone?"

"I know you don't," Matt said, glancing around the room for some support. "But it's like I said the other day, your friend is lost."

Oddly enough, given the conversation leading up to this, Leah's name hadn't yet been mentioned. All Bill and Richard had said was, "We saw her. We saw her right out there." And from the corner, where she hovered watching, Leah wondered who they were talking about.

"She needs to make a transition," Matt explained further, apparently the only one convinced of this, since no one else was agreeing with him. "And the sooner the better."

Bethann stared out into the arena again.

"Maybe if the barns were gone," Matt suggested "Maybe if the arena were torn down."

Bethann turned in a panic. "W-Wh-Why?"

"Because she's going along as usual, and nothing's going to change unless something *does* change."

Richard looked at Christine. She was gazing down at her hands. "It seems so cruel though," she said.

Bill nodded. "And what if you change things and only make her mad?"

Matt considered the possibility for a second or two, and ceased stepping up and down on the bleacher. He pulled a chair up close to Bill and sat down. "Why? Do you think she could be hostile?"

Bill appeared a little taken aback, Matt was right in his face. "I don't know. I just mentioned it because, as mixed up as she is..." He hesitated, glancing at Bethann. "I mean, she's going around like she's still alive, and the place is empty."

Leah looked around.

Everyone looked around.

"I mean, face it," Bill said. "She's dead, and she doesn't know it. Leah Oliver's dead, and she has no idea."

Leah covered her mouth. Dead? Her? Why would he say such a thing? And just when for some godawful reason she was starting to trust him. Today, of all days. Tuesday.

"So what are we supposed to do?"

Leah fled. She didn't want to know. She'd heard enough.

"We have to make her leave."

Richard drew a breath and sighed. "Which brings us back to square one. How?"

"Maybe if we brought in a medium?" Matt suggested.

"No!" Richard said flatly. "No hocus-pocus!"

Matt frowned at Richard's terminology and skepticism. "It is a viable option."

"No, it's not," Richard said, rising slowly and walking across the room. "Not at all, because let's not forget who we're dealing with here. Leah was a loner."

Matt nodded. "Good point." Her personality just might be the key. He turned to Bethann. She would know better than anyone. "Talk to me," he said. "Tell me what you're thinking."

Bethann hesitated. She always stuttered more when she was the center of attention, and everyone was looking at her. "I'm th-think-ing that t-t-tearing the barns d-d-down, isn't g-g-going to make her l-l-leave at all. There's m-m-more to M-M-Maple Dale than j-j-just the barns."

"Okay. Then what do you think's keeping her here?"

"I d-d-don't know."

"But you must, Bethann. You must. Think about her just before she died, a few days before. Was there a change in her?"

Bethann shook her head, and answered with her voice quivering. "No, she was th-the s-s-same. Only m-maybe just s-s-sadder. And I d-d-don't think it's r-r-right talking about her l-like sh-she's crazy. Because s-sh-she wasn't. She was my f-f-friend."

Matt smiled inside. "I wasn't insinuating she was crazy, Bethann. God forbid I even acknowledge such a term in my profession. What I was getting at..."

"It's th-the horses," Bethann said."I th-think it's the h-h-horses."

Matt nodded thoughtfully. "All right. Why?"

"Because." Bethann drew a deep breath. "Because if I w-w-were Leah, I w-w-would worry about them. She p-probably wonders where they're at. I've b-b-been t-trying to l-l-let her know that Shad and P-P-Phoenix are okay, but..."

Bill shifted his weight, which caught Matt's eye, and he turned. "Yes?"

Bill shrugged.

"Come on, what are you thinking?" Matt persisted.

He was thinking that Matt was a real pain in the ass, even if he was trying to help. "I think I agree."

"That it's the horses?"

Bill nodded. "Yeah."

"Why?"

"Because of the barn doors. They're always closed in the morning. And gates are open certain times of the day. I got my men thinking I do it for one reason or another, but..."

Christine thought about yesterday, how Bill had behaved when they'd asked his men about the cat, and then about the way he was when Bethann asked him where to put the sign. He didn't want his men to know. It wasn't that they were bothering them, or that he thought the sign was a dumb idea. He just didn't want them to know.

She looked at him differently, and had to wonder how many other times she'd misinterpreted him.

"All right," Matt said. "Let's say it is the horses. How can we assure her they're okay?"

Bethann's eyes lit up. "We c-can bring th-th-them back."

Richard shook his head. That was out of the question and she knew it.

"Well, w-what about just Persian S-S-Son then? What about j-j-just him? Mom'll b-b-be here."

Richard looked at Christine.

"Honey," she said. "I don't see where bringing him back will..."

"But s-s-she'll know he-he-he's fine then. She'll see that h-h-he's okay. Come on, Mom, we h-have t-t-to try something. We h-have to."

Matt turned to Bill. "Would a horse be in the way?"

Bill shook his head.

"Then what do we have to lose?"

Nothing. At least nothing anyone could think of at the moment, so it was settled. Persian Son was coming home, and Bethann was ecstatic. Richard said he would make arrangements to have him shipped tomorrow.

"But what if it doesn't work? What'll we do then?"

"Something else," Matt said matter-of-factly, and after a moment, "You know, I make my living off affairs of the heart. Attached to a brain in most cases, but affairs of the heart nonetheless. And yet I never cease to be amazed." What amazed him was how people could come together, for whatever the reason, some tragic and some just by circumstance. But coming together, pulling together. Together. "Here's a woman, who besides Bethann, you hardly knew. And yet..."

Tears welled up in Christine's eyes. True, they had hardly known Leah, but Leah was a part of them now. A part of her. An important part.

"Why do you suppose that is?" Matt asked, looking at Richard.

Richard shook his head. Christine hated showing her emotions, no one knew that better than him, and he felt helpless. He couldn't go to her. He couldn't put his arms around her. He couldn't comfort her. He couldn't do anything. He could only sit there. "I don't know."

Matt turned to Christine, and was about to ask her next, but Bill intervened. For Christ sake, couldn't he see she was crying. "What difference does it make?" he said. "As long as they do."

Matt smiled. "None. None whatsoever," he said, repeating, "as long as they do."

And Bill just had.

"But humor me," Matt said.

Christine wiped her eyes and they all glanced at each other and laughed. "I think it's because..." she said, hesitating.

When Matt motioned for her to continue, she looked at Richard. "I think it's because in our own way, we can relate to what a person is going through, what Leah was going through. Because when you love something, the way she loved Maple Dale, and you think it's yours..." Her voice cracked, and she had to clear her throat. "When someone takes that away from you. When someone says it isn't yours anymore..."

Richard swallowed hard.

"Then you have nothing. You don't know what to do. You don't know where to go."

Richard mouthed the words, "I'm sorry." He'd said it before, many, many times. "I'm sorry, Christine."

But sorry didn't take away the pain, not for Christine as least. She wished to God it could. "And if Leah died this way, feeling so helpless, feeling so lost..."

Matt looked at Bill. "What about you? What do you think?"

Bill glanced at Richard, and then Christine and Bethann. "I think we're all afraid of being lost."

"And?"

The lump in Bill's throat made it difficult to speak. He felt bad for Richard. And he felt bad for Christine. For whatever they were going through.

"Do you think because of that then," Matt said, "that we become obligated to help somehow?"

"No." Bill shook his head. "Not obligated. It's just hoping that someone would do the same for you. That if you were lost..."

Richard nodded slowly. "That's it. That someone would do the same for you. One and the same."

Klaus activated his garage door opener, and once inside, waited for it to close completely before getting out of his car. Someone had been following him, and he'd had to drive around for hours before feeling safe enough to go home.

His house was cozy though, it was his haven, even now as he constantly looked over his shoulder. And in his den, was his favorite chair. Mahogany and leather.

It felt good to be home, so good, and he basked in that feeling for a moment, just sitting there. Then he looked around the room. The windows. He wondered if he'd been successful in losing whoever it was that had been following him, and got up and closed the drapes and poured himself a drink. It burned his throat.

What a day.

He sat back down and leaned forward to take off his shoes, but couldn't bend over far enough to see what he was doing, and ended up kicking them off.

"Who would be following me anyway?"

He stomped his feet in anger, shouting, "Who? Who goddammit! Who?" over and over, again and again and again, until his pulse pounded in his head, then leaned back and stared at the ceiling. His hand curled around his drink. He held it loosely at first, then tightly, loose then tight, loose then tight. He wanted to hurl it across the room. It was his, he could do it, he owned it, but the glass was fine lead crystal, imported, and he bought it to his mouth instead. It burned less now.

His answering machine lay just beyond his fingertips, the correct distance for a change after constantly yelling at his housekeeper about it. Another drink and he turned it on. There were eight messages. Only one interested him. The one from Richard.

"Call me, there's something going on at Maple Dale I need to talk to you about."

"Fuck Maple Dale!" he said. "Fuck it! Fuck it! Fuck it!" And thus said, a smile slowly spread across his face.

"Yeah, that's what I'll do."

He turned his machine off, and walked down the hall to his bedroom. There lay his bed, waiting. His pulse quickened as he ran his eyes over it, welcoming him, reminding him of all the self-gratification, and how good it felt. How precise. How exact.

He undressed quickly and got under the covers. This was going to be the best. The absolute best. The ultimate. Maple Dale was his. He could do anything he wanted to with it. But when he slid his hand down to his erect penis, his anticipation turned to horror.

"Oh my God!"

He hadn't washed his hands.

He'd forgotten.

And they were dirty.

Terribly dirty.

-Fourteen-

LEAH WANDERED through the woods, clutching Phoenix to her chest. She'd never thought much about death, and had never believed in an afterlife where one would enter through pearly gates adorned with seraphims and cherubims. But she never expected to be this alone either.

Alone, and losing more of herself everyday. She looked down at what was left, and wondered how she could remain standing. But of course. It was Maple Dale. Her precious Maple Dale. Even in her death, she could depend on it. And she still had Phoenix, at least he was alive. Wasn't he? Yes. He had to be, she could hear him purring. So maybe death wasn't so bad. I can live with this, she thought. I can.

She raised her eyes to the sky. What a notion anyway, God. It was just clouds and shades of blue. Clouds that formed vague shapes which dissipated into nothing.

Nothing.

No warmth. No direction. No recognition.

Nothing.

Richard was about to leave his office for the day, when his secretary buzzed him and announced that Klaus Bukener was there to see him. He glanced at his watch and sighed. He wanted to get home and talk to Christine. "All right, send him in."

Klaus darted his eyes around the room upon entering. "I had to be in the area, so..."

Richard motioned for him to have a seat, and sat back in amazement at how much weight Klaus had gained. He even waddled when he walked. Then, which totally blew Richard's mind, before sitting down the man made the sign of the cross.

The sign of the cross. At first it looked like he was just scratching his forehead, then his chest, and finally both shoulders. All in a flurry. A blur. "So when I got your message on my answering machine." Another sign of the cross. "I wondered what you were trying to pull now."

"I'm not trying to *pull* anything," Richard said. "I just wanted to let you know what we're doing."

Klaus eyed him suspiciously.

"Last night, Bill and I saw Leah."

Klaus sprang to his feet. "Saw her?! What do you mean you saw her? I knew it! You and that nigger are nuts!"

Never in Richard's life, did the word nigger sound so vulgar. He rose then too, with a hardened gaze, and reached for his briefcase. "Why don't you call me and make an appointment."

"I thought you said it was important!"

"It was, and it is," Richard said, glaring. "But I don't have time for you right now."

Klaus exploded. "You don't have time for me?!" Another sign of the cross. "Who do you think you are?! You know, I've been pretty cooperative with you until now. But if need be..."

Richard slammed his briefcase down on the desk. It sounded like a gun blast. "Don't threaten me, Klaus. Don't even think about threatening me! I'll hang you out to dry. You *and* the zoning committee. Do you understand?

Klaus took a step back, bumping into the chair, and frightened, swung around to see who was behind him.

No one.

"I uh..." His tone changed. "I'm sorry. Truly I am. And I *was* out of line, you're right." Another sign of the cross. He wondered how Richard had found out about the zoning board. Who told him? Who hadn't he paid enough? "Please..."

Richard just stood there.

"You said you were going to be doing something at Maple Dale. What? I need to know what?"

Richard drew a deep breath. If only the man weren't so... "I'm bringing my daughter's horse back for a while. We got to talking about it this morning and think it's a good idea. We think it might enable Leah's spirit to..."

Klaus's expression changed. "Did you really see her? I mean really?"

Richard nodded. "Yes. We did. And while I don't plan on getting into this with you right now, we've decided..."

"Who decided? You said *we*. Who's we?"

Richard hesitated. The man was crossing himself again.

"Who?"

Richard just looked at him a second. "My daughter, Christine and Bill, and I have since talked to Walter and..."

"Who else?" Klaus asked, before Richard could finish. "Who else? Have you talked to someone else?"

"Yes," Richard said, shaking his head in amazement. "A friend of mine. Matt Campbell."

Klaus gasped. "Matt Campbell?"

Richard nodded. "Yes. Why? Do you know him?"

"No." Sign of the cross. "I never heard of him."

Richard's being late reminded Christine of all the other times he'd been late, back when he used to call with excuses. Excuses she'd believed. It seemed so long ago, and yet as if it were yesterday. When Bethann came into the kitchen, she found her mother staring painfully out the window.

"Did D-D-Dad call?"

Christine forced a smile, one that said no but that there's nothing to worry about, and Bethann headed for the back door. "I'm g-g-gonna take Shad for a w-w-walk." He wagged his tail at her side. "He w-w-won't let me b-be."

"Don't be long. It's getting dark."

Bethann told her she was only going as far as the corner, and on the way back, was surprised to see her mother out by the wood pile.

"Come grab an armful," Christine called to her. "We'll make a fire."

"A f-f-fire?" Bethann's eyes widened. "Do y-y-you know h-h-how?"

Christine started past her with a hefty bundle. "Sure, come on. How hard can it be anyway?"

Bethann laughed, and between the two of them, they managed. Richard came home and found them stretched out in front of it on the floor in the den with Shad.

"Where's the camera?" he teased. "We're talking Christmas cards here."

Christine smiled and sat up, yawning as Bethann chuckled. "Neat, h-h-huh?"

Richard nodded and sat down, gazing at Christine. "Beautiful. Just beautiful."

"We g-g-got tired of waiting f-f-for you Where w-w-were you? Why d-d-didn't you c-call?"

Richard smiled. Oh, to be young again and so direct. "Klaus came in to see me right as I was getting ready to leave."

Shad got up and meandered over to rest his head on Richard's knee. "And how are you today?" Richard asked.

Shad wagged his tail.

"You don't say?"

Christine smiled, watching them, but glanced away when Richard looked up. "We *were* getting worried."

"I'm sorry. I should've called."

Christine shrugged, with tears suddenly welling up in her eyes, and Richard turned to Bethann. "Get me something to drink, honey," he said, and when she bounced out of the room, "Christine..."

"I'm sorry." She wiped her eyes. "I seem to be doing this a lot lately. But I was just thinking..." She hesitated. "I was thinking about how you used to always call, which I thought was so considerate, when all along..."

Richard swallowed hard.

"And now you don't call, and..."

Richard shook his head. "I'll never hurt you like that again, Christine. I promise."

"I know," she said. "I know."

When Bethann returned with a glass of iced tea, Christine managed to sound in complete control, said she was going to check on dinner, and left the room.

A minute later, Matt tapped on the kitchen door. "Me again," he said. "Can Richard come out to play?"

Christine dried up what was left of her tears. "No, we're just about to eat. Would you like to join us? We're having chili."

"I don't know," he said. Big decision. "That depends. Did you use lean meat?"

"Yes."

"Then I'd love to," Matt said, lifting the lid to see for himself. "But only three quarters of a cup."

Christine rolled her eyes. "Would you like me to measure it?"

"If you don't mind."

Christine laughed.

After dinner, and when Christine and Bethann left the kitchen, Richard told Matt about his meeting with Klaus, strange behavior included.

"Did he and Leah get along?" Matt asked.

"I don't know. It's obvious she got along well with his father, considering the provision he made for her in his will. But him, I don't know. Why?"

"No reason." Matt shrugged. "I was just curious."

Richard smiled. *Just* curious. "So anyway, it's all set. Persian Son'll be back tomorrow."

Matt nodded and walking over to leave then, stopped at the door. "Keep me posted."

Richard said he would, and Matt studied him for a moment. "Why don't you take a walk with me. You look like you could use some fresh air."

Richard called to Christine and told her he'd be back in a little while. They took Shad with them, and walked in silence for some time.

"How's Christine?" Matt asked.

Richard glanced at him. "I was hoping you'd be able to tell me."

Matt smiled faintly. He wished he could. "I think this is taking a toll on her. It's difficult enough for anyone to handle, but she's relating to Leah as a woman. A woman who died lonely."

Richard stared down at the sidewalk. "Is she ever going to forgive me, Matt?"

"I don't know. It's hard to say. Have you forgiven yourself?"

Richard shook his head.

"Then why are you expecting something from her, that you yourself..."

"I love her, Matt."

"She knows that, Richard."

"And I keep trying to show her that I'll never do anything like that again. But at the same time, she can't forget." Richard swallowed hard. "She can't. I see it in her eyes every time she looks at me."

"And what does she see when she looks at you?" Matt asked. "What does she see in your eyes?"

Richard's voice cracked. "A man that hurt her. A man that screwed up."

"Right," Matt said softly. "A constant reminder."

Richard stared out into the night.

"Do you understand what I'm saying?"

Richard nodded.

"I'll see you tomorrow."

When Richard got back to the house, he let Shad in, and sat down on the porch and gazed up at the stars. Christine checked on him after a while.

"What are you doing?"

He shrugged. "Just thinking."

"Okay." She smiled and started to shut the door.

"Christine..."

She hesitated.

"Why don't you come sit with me?"

"It's cold out here."

"I'll give you my jacket."

She laughed. "That's not necessary." She had one by the door, and put it on as she came out and sat down.

They were quiet for a few minutes. "Thinking about Maple Dale?" she asked.

Richard shook his head. "No, I was thinking about us."

Christine stared down at her hands.

"I was thinking about how I want back in your life," he said.

Tears welled up in Christine's eyes, and she moved to get up, but he stopped her. "I don't want to live like this anymore, Christine. I can't."

She nodded. Neither could she. "I keep trying. I'm trying so hard. If only I could forget..."

"You can't, Christine. You can't. And neither can I. But that has to say something too. Only for God sake, don't let it say that we..." Richard's voice trembled. "I love you, Christine."

He turned her face to his, his voice but a whisper now. "Let me back in your life."

Time stood still as he searched her eyes, the tears spilling down her cheeks. The pain. The anguish. Forgiveness. She nodded then, smiling faintly, and he leaned toward her slowly and kissed her, for the first time in fourteen months.

"I love you, Richard," she said.

He kissed her again.

"And I'm sorry too."

-Fifteen-

LEAH WATCHED as Maple Dale flourished, and so enjoyed herself, that at times she even forgot about being dead. She was like a child at a fair, a circus, gazing, taking everything in as she followed Bill from one event to the next. She liked being near him. He was always humming, and he was meticulous in everything he did. This pleased her greatly, his being as fussy as she was about the way things were done. But more importantly, he made her feel safe.

Phoenix had also taken a liking to him, and although he normally kept his distance, Leah would have to scold him occasionally when he came too close. Nothing could hurt her anymore, especially this black man, but Phoenix was alive and still needed to be cautious.

Persian Son's arrival was a dream come true. She loved watching him *act up* in the paddock. Bill seemed to get a kick out of it too, though he wasn't quite comfortable with him yet. She could see that. But he was kind, and that was more important. Respect and kindness. Horses sense that.

With Thanksgiving only a few weeks away, the onset of what Matt with tongue-in-cheek referred to as the holiday rush, jogging time was getting scarce. He took it whenever he could, and was just about to sneak out between appointments for a few extra miles, when a large figure of a man came in the door, backwards.

Hmph, Matt thought.

The man glanced over his shoulder, and when the door closed, turned. "You Dr. Campbell?"

Matt nodded. The man was a wreck.

"I'm Klaus Bukener."

Obviously.

"We need to talk."

Matt glanced at his secretary's empty desk. It was lunch time.

"I don't need an appointment," Klaus said. "This won't take long."

Matt showed him into his office.

"Can you leave the door open?"

Matt nodded, making a mental note of the request, and motioned for him to have a seat.

Klaus remained standing. "First of all," he said. "Let me tell you, I don't believe in any of this bullshit about a ghost up at Maple Dale."

Matt sat down at his desk. "You mean Leah Oliver's ghost?"

"Anybody's ghost!" Klaus spat.

"I see," Matt said. "Then why are you here?"

"Why? Because I believe you started this."

Matt motioned again for him to have a seat and, studying him when he finally did, noticed his hands. "That's interesting, Mr. Bukener. But tell me, do you have an objection to all ghosts, or just Leah Oliver's?"

Klaus refused to answer that. "I want you to put a stop to it. I want you to call it off."

Matt nodded nonchalantly. "Sure thing. I'll just wave my magic wand."

Klaus sneered. "Is this how you normally fix your patient's problems? By mocking them?"

"Wait a minute," Matt said. "In the first place, you're not my patient. Secondly, I don't *fix* anyone's problems. Therapy is a combined effort."

"Yeah, and *you* get paid."

Matt glanced at the man's hands again. "It's a living. What about you?"

Klaus narrowed his beady eyes. "What do you mean?"

"Making money," Matt said. "Isn't that the name of the game?"

Klaus shrugged. "My father thought so."

Matt nodded slowly, studying him again, and motioned to his hands. They were raw. "What happened to your hands?"

"Nothing. They're fine."

"They don't look fine."

"I *said* they're fine."

"All right." Matt sat back, waiting. "So now what?"

"Now what?! I already told you why I came here!"

Matt nodded. "And I'm supposed to do something about her ghost."

"There is no ghost! I told you I don't believe in that shit!"

Matt sighed impatiently. "And yet..."

"Why did you get involved anyway? You never even knew her!"

"True."

"So why do you care?"

"I don't know. Why do you care?"

"I don't!"

"What about your father?"

"What about him?"

"Did he care?"

Klaus clammed up.

"I'm sorry. Does it bother you, the relationship she had with your father?"

"Bother me? Does it *bother* me?!" Klaus jumped to his feet, his eyes bulging. "What relationship? They didn't have a relationship! Don't you see? They didn't need anyone! Neither one of them! Oh sure, father had his women. God knows he was always beating his rod somewhere! But *needing* someone? No! Never!"

With this, the encounter came to an end. Klaus stormed from the room, looking over his shoulder. And after sitting there for a while, thinking, Matt phoned a colleague, then Richard.

"Are you aware of the exact cause of Leah's death?" he asked.

"Yes, heart failure," Richard said. "Why?"

"Because there's more to it than that."

"What do you mean?"

"I mean, her heart burst. Richard, she died of a broken heart. And not only that, according to the Coroner's report, there wasn't a mark on her."

"The *Coroner's* report?"

"Yes. Klaus Bukener paid me a visit today, with hands that have been washed a thousand times. Guilty hands."

"Wait a minute."

"I can't. I don't have time. But tell me, didn't you say that Bethann and some of the other students found her in the barn on the cement floor?"

"Yes."

"Then doesn't it seem odd that she didn't have any bruises anywhere from the fall?"

Richard's blood drained from his face. "Are you implying Klaus had something to do with her death?"

"I don't know. What do you think?"

Leah kept a vigilant eye on Bethann as she warmed up Persian Son. She had an audience inside as well, Christine, Walter, and Richard, and she was enjoying the attention. So much so, that like most adolescents, the attention went to her head. Waving, as if to say *watch this,* she started toward the in-and-out set of jumps, but took the turn much too tight and with a loose rein. Persian Son, consequently, even being the veteran that he was and fully capable of taking the jump on his own, dropped his shoulder at the last second, and ducked out on it.

Bethann almost landed on the ground.

"Serves you right!" To the untrained eye, Persian Son was just being a handful, and rather exciting to watch. But Leah had a fit. "You weren't even looking at the jump until the last second, and off half a stride! What did you think you were doing?"

Bethann blushed bright red. She could practically hear Leah in her mind, knowing exactly what she would say, what she was saying. She circled the arena, in hand, focused, and took the jumps beautifully. "Yes! Much better!"

Bill came into the office and joined everyone watching. Soon though, it was back to business. Richard had been in negotiation with Klaus and Leah's lawyers, and passed along the news.

Walter was elated. "Then this means we can sell some lots?"

Richard nodded, smiling. He had mixed feelings about going ahead, but compromising at this point allowed them what they'd decided for Leah's sake. "Everything except for the lots in this area." He circled the arena, barns, and paddocks on Walter's map. "These remain unattainable for the time being."

Klaus's house was right in the middle of the circle, but there was nothing that could be done about that. He was still insisting on his intent to move there upon completion.

M a p l e   D a l e

Bethann came in after cooling out Persian Son and was filled in on the latest developments. Her father had told her this was more than likely. He'd explained it all to her, yet met with the same resistance.

"What w-w-will Leah th-think, with p-people looking around and t-t-talking?"

Richard sighed. He couldn't stop thinking about what Matt had said, not exactly something he could use to stop legal process. But once Matt put a thought into your head...

"Honey, for all we know she's gone. There hasn't been a lot of..." Richard's voice trailed off as he looked at Bill. She *wasn't* gone. "Did you see her again?"

Bill shook his head. "No, but I can feel her. She's still here."

Richard glanced at Christine, who gave him one of her what-do-we-do-now looks, and he smiled, thinking about the past few weeks, making love and holding on to each other.

Bethann's impatience quickly brought him back to the matter at hand. She was glad her mom and dad were together again, it felt good. But as is also rather typical of adolescence, she had taken it for granted already. "But w-what if th-they scare her?"

"We've got some time, don't worry. She's obviously been content lately, or we'd have seen some signs. So let's make her happier. Remember what Matt said?"

Bethann nodded. Matt said her personality was the key, and to think about what would make *her* happy. "Let's p-p-put her tack back in th-the tack room. She was r-r-really p-particular about her t-t-tack."

Richard exchanged glances with Walter and Bill, one shrugged, the other nodded. Bill thought it was a good idea, so that's what they did. Less than a half hour later, Leah's saddle, bridles, hard hat, and schooling chaps, were back in their customary places. Bethann walked away with a satisfied smile. Leah would be pleased, she knew she would. And she was. That night, after everyone had gone and the barn was all quiet except for the sounds of Persian Son nestling in his straw, she went into the tack room and looked around.

"Perfect," she said. It was as if she were alive. Her bridles were hung in figure eighths, the neck strap wrapped around and through the reins. Her saddle was covered with the sheepskin pad, the way she always left it to dry, and her chaps were hung by the door.

She saw a room full of bridles and saddles, and in passing Persian Son, saw a stable of horses. Shad was fine, the sign in the hayloft reminded her of that, and Phoenix was free to roam. "Perfect."

Over the next two weeks, the second floor was roughed-in on Klaus's home, three building lots were sold, Bethann passed all her quarterly exams, she'd had her doubts, and Maple Dale, along with all of northeast Ohio, received its first measurable snowfall of the season.

With Thanksgiving fast approaching, Walter, Christine, and Bill discussed their holiday plans. Bill was looking forward to having dinner at his favorite aunt's and watching football all day. Christine talked about having dinner at home, what she was making, who all was coming, all the shopping she had to do. And Walter and his family were driving to upstate New York to ski.

Leah watched and listened from the corner, with Phoenix directly above her, sleeping in the rafters. Holidays meant nothing to her. They never had. She was always alone. But she enjoyed listening to them planning theirs, and envisioned it, the turkey, the dressing, the sweet potatoes...

Bill said something to Walter about digging three more wells up on the north end, and Christine told him about a young couple interested in a certain lot, and how she had to double talk, so as not to let on there was any problem.

"Did they buy it?" Bill asked.

Christine nodded. "For the time being, yes."

Leah didn't understand.

"But come spring," Walter said, "when the barn's leveled and a house goes up..."

"Right. How do we explain it then?"

Leah clutched her chest. "Oh no! It's still happening! They're destroying Maple Dale!"

Dust whirled suddenly, whirled and whirled, rattling the windows and quaking the walls. The lights blinked. The cat ran. And as Christine, Bill, and Walter turned in horror, the door flew open.

"Oh my God!" Walter gasped. "She was here and overheard us! She knows!"

Christine looked helplessly at Bill. There was such sadness in his eyes, such despair. Later that afternoon, Leah's anger manifested itself. Lunch boxes came up missing, hammers were broken, tires were flattened, and tractor keys disappeared.

Bill sent his men home early, wanting to get them out of there before her activities were actually witnessed by someone, and a meeting was set at Christine's for later that day to decide what to do.

-Sixteen-

THEY HAD no sooner assembled, Matt included, when Walter started blaming himself. "Everything was fine till I opened my big mouth."

Christine passed pumpkin bread around. "We were *all* talking, Walter, so..."

"Besides," Matt said. "Things obviously weren't fine. You just brought it to a head. She's no closer to leaving now than she was before."

Walter shook his head. "But she's been quiet. She could've been doing things, and she hasn't."

"Complacence," Matt said, and drew a deep breath. "Complacence." Everyone was quiet for a moment. No one knew what to say. "Ours, as well as hers."

Silence.

It was true.

"Even if we could change everything back to the way it was, the horses, the students, all of it. Looking at it now, do you think she'd leave?"

No, they decided. Not judging from her recent behavior. If she'd become content...

Christine sighed. "It's a shame we can't have it both ways. Enough of the old to make her feel secure, but enough of the new to..."

Everyone nodded in agreement, even Bethann. But agreeing on *what* to do was a different thing. Whatever they decided, had to be drastic.

"Had you planned on working throughout the winter there?" Matt asked Bill after a while.

"About half my crew, yes. Why?"

"I was just wondering how much it would hurt to pull out entirely."

Walter's eyes widened. "Indefinitely, or for just a short time?"

"I don't know. A week, maybe two, a month, what with Thanksgiving and Christmas coming."

"Why?" Richard asked. "What's the point? It was shut down before and didn't accomplish anything."

"I know. But I mean *completely*. Barricades in the driveway, no electricity, everything."

"You m-mean even P-P-Persian Son?" Bethann asked.

Matt nodded. "Even Persian Son." He was thinking that if Leah had absolutely no reason whatsoever to stay, then maybe she'd finally face the reality of there being nothing here for her anymore. "And for her sake, I think we have to do it."

Richard phoned Klaus the following morning, left a message on the answering machine, and they proceeded as planned. Walter and Christine cleaned out their desks. The contents of the tack room and store room were taken to Richard and Christine's garage. The construction equipment was moved to another site. Persian Son was shipped back to Manchester Farms. The pipes were drained and the utilities were turned off. All that was left was Phoenix.

He was everywhere, everywhere they looked. Watching, purring, stretching, licking his paws and yawning. Fortunately, Bethann had been excluded from this part of the plan, and even now, Bill and Richard hesitated going through with it.

"It has to be done though," Richard said. He and Bill both agreed on that. But looking at him now, curled up in a little gray ball at the end of the barn, it seemed so cruel.

Bill sighed. "I just hate to think of him roaming around here cold and hungry. He's grown to depend on us, you know."

Richard nodded. Everyone was gone and it was just them now. The two of them, and Phoenix.

And Leah. She'd been watching them for some time, wondering what was going on, and now hovered near so she could hear what they were saying.

They'd discussed the issue well into the night about what to do, and why. Funny how it came down to him, a cat not much bigger than a kitten.

"Don't let his size fool you," Matt had said. "He'll find his way. But *not* if you leave the food. He can get water by the lake."

"Yeah, until it freezes over."

Bill and Richard stood staring at him, no more than ten, fifteen feet away. "You want to try catching him again?"

Richard shrugged, raising an eyebrow, and with that, the two of them started toward him.

Leah screamed! It sounded like the wind. And Phoenix bolted.

Bill and Richard froze. Leah was close by. They couldn't see her, but they could feel her. She was everywhere. In front of them, in back of them. Everywhere.

"Now what?" Richard whispered.

Bill gave him a look, a high-sign of sorts, and started talking. "It's supposed to be a cold winter. Colder than usual."

Richard nodded, understanding. "It's good then that we're closing down."

"Yeah, but like I said, it's a shame about the cat."

"I know." Richard shook his head. "Without food..."

Bill nodded sadly. "If he'd just let us catch him."

Leah clutched her chest.

"It'll be months before someone comes back up here."

"Oh my God!" Leah gasped. "Poor Phoenix!" She swept past them in a gust of wind, and hid in the corner of the hayloft. The sign Bethann left had been a lie. "A lie!" she cried, petting Phoenix desperately and cradling him tight. "A lie! What am I going to do?"

Richard and Bill hesitated, then walked out and closed the barn door behind them. They'd done all they could.

Tears filled Leah's eyes as she rocked back and forth. "Oh my God! How will I feed you? How will I keep you warm?"

Phoenix purred against her heart.

"How?"

She heard a car start.

"Oh my God!"

Then a truck.

"They're leaving you!"

Phoenix nuzzled her face, as she frantically looked around, seeing what she had to offer. Nothing but her love. It wouldn't be enough. He'd be cold. He'd be hungry.

She hurried down the loft and threw open the door. Richard and Bill were standing by Bill's truck.

"Go with them!"

She put him down, and turned, but he followed her.

"I said go!" Leah cried. "Please! I can't take care of you! Don't you understand? I can't take care of you!"

Richard and Bill watched in anguish. Phoenix kept turning around, and would get shoved back. He was crying. Then the barn door closed, and he was left on the outside.

Bill walked over and picked him up, shivering, his little chest pounding, and handed him to Richard. It broke their hearts, this tiny little cat, the way he looked up at them. Two grown men, with tears in their eyes.

"Jesus, what this must be doing to her," Bill said.

Richard nodded, his voice quivering. "I know." And long after they'd gone, Leah stared down the hill at the path they'd taken, all alone now. Totally.

-Seventeen-

CHRISTINE INSISTED Phoenix visit the veterinarian before settling in, and after being assured he was in good health, allowed him full run of the house. Bethann loved him. He was definitely *her* cat. But as happy as she was to have him home, she was sure this wasn't the way for Leah to pass on. And even if it was, she was afraid she'd be leaving more hurt than she'd been before.

Richard had his doubts also, and was formulating another plan just in case. Being very careful not to overlook even the slightest detail, he and Bethann worked tirelessly in the basement workshop for hours on end. "My humble assistant and her dad," he called them. They wanted it to be a surprise, so Christine wasn't allowed downstairs.

Over the next few weeks, what fears Christine had about Phoenix, vanished. He and Shad constantly entertained them with their antics, and many times she found herself just watching them and laughing. She couldn't imagine the two of them separated, and often, was close to tears just thinking about it. She was becoming as sentimental as her mother.

Heaven forbid, she thought, just like her.

A northern storm front combined with the lake-effect dumped thirteen inches of snow across the area, with a promise of that much more to come within the next twelve hours. Schools were closed, parking bans were activated, and all the local ski areas were packed, despite temperatures hovering in the single digits.

With endless time, Leah's existence closed in on her. The long days gave way to even longer nights as the windows frosted over, and she was beginning to think of Maple Dale as her tomb, her hell on earth. More and more, she wished she'd had the foresight to have seen it coming, to have known. But these thoughts were always followed by the ones where she was sure nothing would have changed anyway. Even if her life had been different, fate is fate, she'd tell herself. That's just how it is.

Then there were times, when it was too quiet and she couldn't even hear the wind, when she would think about the things that meant the most to her. The things that were gone, the things that were still there, the things that didn't matter anymore. Things. That's all they were. Because without the students and their laughter, without the horses, and without the caring, they were nothing. Maple Dale was nothing.

She missed Phoenix. He'd provided her with the only warmth she'd felt since her death. Her heart ached for him, ached beyond words, though never did she question her decision to push him away. It was something she had to do. She knew that then, and she knew that now. Still, there were times when she would cry fitfully for him, and found herself wondering if this was how her mother felt when she'd given her away.

Three weeks from the day Maple Dale was shut down, Richard met Bill and Walter there. It was cold, bitter cold, and the drive hadn't

M a p l e   D a l e

been plowed, so they had to trudge up the hill on foot. They felt like they were climbing Mount Everest.

They'd come to see if there were any signs of Leah's presence, to see if maybe she'd finally passed on. They didn't have to look long. When they opened the door to the office, they startled her, dust swirled, and they felt her go right through them, in spite of their many layers of clothing.

She was still there.

No doubt about it.

They left without saying a word, and Leah hurried to the window to rub a spot in the frosted glass so she could watch them walk back down the hill.

At the bottom, they turned to one another. "Now what?" Something had to be decided.

"I'll try to get a hold of Klaus again," Richard said, suggesting another meeting that evening. When he arrived home, Christine was baking cookies.

Sugar cookies.

Yesterday it was chocolate chip, the day before that, butterballs and crescents, before that, pecan twirls, thumbprints, and before that, crisscross peanut butter. Dozens and dozens of them.

"Wow! What's on the agenda for tomorrow?" Richard teased, helping himself to a few.

"Nothing." Christine wiped her brow. "With this batch, I'm done." And with four days yet till Christmas.

Richard smiled, just gazing at her for a moment, then grew serious. "She's still there."

"Did you see her?"

"No." Richard shook his head. "But we felt her. She's so cold."

Tears filled Christine's eyes instantly. She didn't ask how do you know? What makes you say that? Are you sure? She only asked, "What are we going to do now?" Because just the thought of Leah being cold...

"I don't know." Richard told her about Bill and Walter coming over later, and said he was going to call Matt and Klaus as well. "We'll talk about it then."

Matt was first to arrive, dressed like an Eskimo and boasting of breaking his all-time record for a five-mile run in the snow, "By nine whole seconds! On the dot!"

Christine smiled.

"I smelled your kitchen clear down the block!"

Christine laughed. "I've had this compulsion to bake lately. Which is all right, I guess, except that I keep eating everything."

"I've noticed," Matt teased, shedding an outer layer of lycra-spandex, and then another. "Right around the middle."

Christine glanced at her figure. He was kidding, but it got her to thinking. Fortunately, just about the time she decided her pants *were* getting snugger in the waist, Bill and Walter arrived to divert her attention.

They all sat down in the den with coffee and a platter of assorted cookies. Shad was stretched out on the rug in front of the fireplace with Bethann. Phoenix meandered about. Bill smiled each time he saw him. He even pet him once, laughing about it. And for a while, it was as if they were just a group of friends gathered for the holiday.

Klaus had told Richard he'd tried to attend, but Richard doubted seriously if he would from the way he'd sounded. He waited until eight. When it was obvious he wasn't coming, he excused himself and went down to the basement to bring up the project he and Bethann had been working on.

It was large, but not heavy, mounted on a piece of plywood, and covered with a sheet. Everyone looked on expectantly as he set it down on the coffee table.

"A while back, at one of these meetings," he said, pausing. "Christine said something that got me to thinking. Something Bethann and I took to heart."

Christine couldn't imagine what, and Bethann explained. "It was wh-when you s-s-said, that it w-w-was a shame that ww-we couldn't have s-s-some of the old, but enough of the nn-new to…" She choked up, unable to finish, and her father put his arm around her. A lump formed in his throat.

"Matt, you said that whatever we did, let it be for Leah's sake. Not ours, but hers. And we tried."

Matt nodded in acknowledgment.

"But Leah's in all of us. Each one of us. So what we do for her, has to be right for everyone, otherwise." Richard swallowed hard. "Otherwise…"

"Otherwise it won't work," Matt said, proud inside. "So what did you come up with?"

"Hopefully the answer," Richard said. When Bethann removed the sheet, they all stared wide-eyed. It was Maple Dale. "The kind of Maple Dale we'd like to see. A Maple Dale that's an equestrian community."

"Well I'll be damned," Bill whispered. "Would you look at this."

It was a scale model. "Close," Richard said, complete with arena, barns, trees, houses, paddocks, the cross country course, and even horses. Eight of them, decked out in bright red horse blankets as they grazed on one of the hills.

Bill shook his head in amazement. "No wonder you've been asking me so many questions about the trees and the streams."

Richard smiled, and glanced at Christine. She was dabbing at her eyes. She obviously approved, immensely. Walter was in awe, envisioning every house, fence, and drive.

"How many streets?"

"That's up to you," Richard said. "We just dotted the houses here and there. I've met with zoning and got a tentative okay on a variation. And as you can see, there's a picnic area here. And over here, we were thinking of maybe one or two tennis courts, and a basketball court here."

Walter glanced up and grinned. "What about a three-hole golf course?"

Richard laughed. "We never thought of that, but why not?"

"Yeah," Bill said, nodding. "Why not?"

Matt sat back and looked from one to the next, wishing to God that Leah could be here, to see how much people really cared.

"Does this change the size of the lots?"

"Some I think," Richard said, "like up here by the barn. We want to take Bethann's third in bits and pieces, so you'll have to work around that. We'd want to keep this pasture here, and of course the barn and the arena, and the cross country course, and the trails that wind up and around this way."

Walter liked the idea more and more as they went along. It'd be similar to buying a condominium, where the residents have access to a pool, tennis courts, and recreation rooms. Only here, they'd have a stable, grounds, and a home of their own. "And with the varying lots, you're open to far more buyers. Not everybody wants three acres."

Bill nodded. They were all in agreement.

"What does Klaus think?"

"I don't know," Richard said. "But I'm hoping since we're not taking Bethann's third cohesively, he won't object."

The following day, Klaus reluctantly agreed to a meeting. "In the town square at one."

The man's crazy, Richard thought, it was freezing out. But Klaus insisted it be there, so town square it was, windchill factor and all. Richard hardly recognized him. He was bundled in an ankle-length overcoat with at least three scarves tied around his neck. He had a hat pulled down over his ears and he was wearing a pair of mittens, his arms held stiff as a board and extended from his sides. He looked like a giant penguin.

"Klaus?"

He nodded, his eyes red and darting in all directions. "What did you want to see me about?"

"I have a proposal about Maple Dale I'd like to..."

"Is it going to cost me?" Klaus asked, interrupting and turning himself completely around so he could see in all directions. "Is it?"

Richard looked at him strangely. "It shouldn't."

"Then fine, do it," Klaus said, turning around and around again and starting to leave.

"Wait! Wait a minute," Richard said. "Let me tell you about it so you can..."

Klaus swiveled back around. "Then tell me!"

Richard hesitated. "Bethann wants her third of Maple Dale spread out through the estate. We want to keep the barn and the arena. We're thinking of an equestrian community."

"Then do it I said! Do what you want! I have to go!"

"But I'm going to need something from you. A handshake if nothing else for Christ sake." When he extended his hand, Klaus literally fell over backwards trying to get away from him.

"Jesus..." Richard reached down to help him, but he started backpedaling, still darting his eyes all around. He rolled onto his knees and elbows then, holding his hands out, and with his chin buried in the snow, started groveling.

"Here." Richard grabbed him by the arm and pulled him to his feet, in spite of himself. "Are you all right?"

Klaus nodded, and stumbled down the street, retching as he ducked into an alley, where vomiting so violently, he lost control of his bowels. By the time he got to his car, he couldn't stand his own stench.

-Eighteen-

LEAH COULD SEE nothing of herself anymore, nothing. She'd faded completely away. I must just be a soul now, she thought, all that's left of me. Fearing she was about to lose that too, she started thinking more and more about her mother and her father, her beginning. And why not, it always came down to them anyway. They were to blame for everything. especially her mother. Always.

She edged back further and further into the corner, gazing around her icy tomb, and wondered what would happen if her mother were to appear in front of her, right then, right now. What would she say to her? Would she ask her the questions that had haunted her all her life? Things like, "How could you have given me away? Didn't you care? Why didn't you ever try to find me? Was I conceived in love? Did my father care about me? Did he tell you to give me away?"

Tears welled up in her eyes. Would she ask all this? Or would she be so excited to finally meet her, that none of that would matter anymore? Would she ask instead, "Why am I so tall? Who do I take after? What color are my father's eyes? Why is my voice so deep and my cheeks always red? How did I get such little feet? What's your favorite time of day? Is it early morning, like mine? And why...?"

A smile chased the tears away as she thought of more and more. A broad smile. "Do you like horses? Do you ride? Does my father ride? Do you believe in God? Do you think there is such a thing? What's your favorite flower? Mine's daffodils. Do you like the rain? I do. I love the way it smells. Do you know my name? It's Leah. My name is Leah."

Klaus's attorney, John Smith, couldn't have been happier about the Maple Dale Equestrian Community theme, and assured Richard he'd meet with Klaus immediately to draw up the agreement. "First thing tomorrow."

Richard came home early that afternoon to share the news, and suggested he and Christine and Bethann go out to dinner to celebrate.

"Come on," he coaxed. "We'll go to Top of The Town. Bethann's never been there, it'll be fun."

Christine rested her head back on the couch and yawned. "But I'm *so* tired."

"Of course, from all that cooking and baking no doubt," Richard said. "You need a break."

Bethann laughed. "Come on, M-Mom. We c-c-can see the lights."

Christine yawned again. "Why don't we just have pizza."

Richard and Christine exchanged curious glances.

"I'll even let you get anchovies. In fact, stop and order it then go to that Christmas tree place across the street."

Richard and Bethann's mouths dropped.

"You're g-g-going to let *us* p-p-pick it out alone?"

Christine laughed. They were right, she'd never trusted them before, always wanting to have the perfect tree. "Go!" she said. "Before I change my mind."

They left in a flash, and upon returning, woke her from a nap, with Shad at her feet and Phoenix cuddled under her arm.

"Wait till you see it," Richard said, kissing her as he set the pizza on the coffee table. "It's eight feet tall."

Christine sat up, gulping. "Eight feet?"

Bethann nodded as she came in with napkins, plates, and Cokes. "And it's s-s-so fat."

Christine shook her head, she should've known better. "Eight feet, and fat."

Richard and Bethann nodded proudly.

"What kind is it?"

Richard glanced at Bethann, and together they shrugged. "I don't know. We didn't ask. It's pretty though, if you don't look at that one flat side."

"A *flat* side?"

Richard nodded nonchalantly, and passed her a piece of pizza, smiling. "For you, my sweet."

Christine sighed.

Bethann could hardly keep a straight face now, she had to stuff her mouth full of pizza to keep from laughing, and Richard changed the subject.

"What do you think about a party out at Maple Dale? A real celebration."

Christine plucked an anchovy off her pizza and fed it to Phoenix. "You mean, open to the public?"

"No, not necessarily. Maybe just us. You know, me, you, Bethann, Bill, and Walter, their families, Matt."

Christine gave the idea some thought while feeding Phoenix another anchovy. "When?"

"Soon," Richard said.

Christine smiled. Soon, meant for Leah's sake, so with that in mind, they decided on Christmas Eve and started making plans. Maple Dale would be all decorated and the menu would be simple, maybe just some party trays, cold cuts and relishes. Christine would take care of the desserts herself, she certainly had more than enough cookies already.

"Well, maybe just a few more." she said. "And some nut roll. And a cake. And some punch."

"Do you th-think Mr. Bukener'll c-c-come?"

"I don't know, honey," Richard said, doubting it. "But we can ask."

There was a lot to be done between now and then. But first things first. The tree. Christine took a deep breath, and went to take a look. Richard and Bethann followed her. They wanted to see her reaction.

It was priceless.

"It's a blue spruce!"

Richard nodded. "A six footer. And the man guaranteed me it was cut just last week. I shook it to death and not one needle dropped. Right?"

Bethann nodded. "And th-the trunk is p-p-perfectly straight. As s-s-straight as an arrow. Look! And it's p-p-perfectly round, no b-bare spots, and it was th-the bluest one."

Christine blushed, smiling. "Am I that hard to please?"

"Yes!" they said, laughing. "You are!"

Klaus hung up the phone after talking to his attorney and hurried back to his chair. He'd pushed it to the center of the room so he could see anyone, anything, everything, coming from all directions, and wrapped himself in a blanket. He'd taken five showers since coming home, his skin was red and peeling. He had sores all over his body that were infected from his incessant scratching. And his hands were swollen to twice their size.

Someone was there, he could hear them. "Who are you?" he shouted. "What do you want?"

He'd been to three different doctors this past week alone, but not one could tell him what was wrong with him. "It's your nerves," one suggested. "Perhaps a tranquilizer."

"The sons of bitches!" They were incompetent. There *was too* something wrong with him. There had to be. His heart raced, pounding so hard it felt like it was going to explode. His wrists throbbed, he could see his blood pumping. And no matter what he tried to eat or drink, it refused to stay down, yet he was still gaining weight.

"Who are you?!"

He darted his eyes around the room, and out of the corner of his eye, thought he saw something scurry across the floor. "What was that?" he gasped.

He saw it on the other side.

"There it is again!"

The phone rang.

He jumped, and ran to answer it, but felt something crawl across his feet, and ran back, dropping his blanket.

"Who is it?! Who's calling me?"

He tucked his feet up, something was crawling under his chair. A bug! Hundreds of bugs! Crawling up the chair and onto his legs, then all over his body.

"Oh my God!" He screamed, swatting at them, swatting until his swollen hands were bloody and dripping. "Oh my God! Help me!"

His own voice responded. "This is Klaus Bukener the Second."

"What?! Oh my God!"

Again, "This is Klaus Bukener the Second."

The tape repeated itself over and over, stuck, then clicked, and with the tone, started at the beginning. "This is Klaus Bukener the Second."

Again and again.

And again.

Leah heard a noise outside and, hurrying to the window, rubbed a circle in the frost and peeked out. It was a plow truck, throwing snow high in the air as it forged its way up the hill. Her heart pounded with excitement.

It was Bill. She knew his truck.

Having stopped by Richard's earlier to pick up the scale model of Maple Dale, he shoveled his way to the door, and brought it in and set it down on one of the desks.

Leah watched from the corner. As he uncovered it and stood gazing down at it, he could feel her presence. "Well, isn't this something," he said, as if to himself.

Leah moved closer.

"A Maple Dale Equestrian Community. I suppose that means you have to own a horse to live here, or like them at least."

Leah gazed at it in wonder. "It must," she said, her voice a gentle breeze. "It must."

Bill nodded. "I'm glad they're saving all these trees. It'd be a shame to have to cut them down."

Leah nodded. "It would."

"This trail here's my favorite."

"Mine too."

"And some new trees can be planted here."

"Good idea."

"And here."

Leah looked up at him. "Oaks?"

Bill nodded. "And maples."

"Yes, sugar maples."

Bill walked away with a smile, and glanced back from the door as Leah reached down and gently adjusted one of the horses blankets. "There now," she said. "There now."

Matt grabbed the phone on the first ring, and clearing his throat, focused on the bedside clock. Ironically, he'd been sleeping for a change. "Hello?"

"Leah's coming to get me."

It was Klaus, he recognized the voice, feeble and threaded as it was.

"She's coming to get me."

Matt sat up and raked his fingers through his hair. "But isn't she out at Maple Dale?"

Silence...

"Klaus?"

"No. She's here. She's been following me. She's everywhere I go."

"What do you think she wants?"

"Who knows?" Klaus said, in a despairing voice. "Who knows?"

Matt got out of bed, reaching for his pants. "You, you must. Why else would she be coming for you?"

"I don't know."

"Klaus, go look in the mirror. Go look and see."

"I can't!"

Matt grabbed a shirt and put it on. "Klaus, is your door locked?"

"Yes."

"Unlock it then."

"I can't! She'll get in that way!"

"No, she won't. It works just the opposite. It'll show her you're not afraid of her. Unlock it. Show her you're not afraid."

"But I am afraid!" Klaus confessed. "I am!"

With that exclamation, the phone went dead.

Matt flew down the stairs, and after looking up Klaus's address, phoned the police and met them there. They banged on the doors, back and front, but got no response, and had to break a window to get inside.

Klaus was sitting in the center of his den, slumped forward in his mahogany and leather chair, unconscious and drooling, naked to the world, with two empty pill containers rolling back and forth at his feet.

— Nineteen —

MOST EVERYONE was at Maple Dale by midday, decorating, when Matt arrived. The bearer of grim news, he poured himself a cup of coffee.

"That's not decaf," Christine warned.

He drank it anyway, down to the last drop.

Richard watched him curiously. "Are you all right?"

Matt shook his head. Leah was there. No one had come right out and said so, but he could tell by the way they were acting, by the way they were doing things, and had to choose his words carefully. "I'm fine. It's Klaus."

"What do you mean?"

Everyone turned.

"He's in the hospital. I committed him."

Leah gasped along with everyone else.

"What?"

"What for?"

"He attempted suicide."

"Suicide?"

Matt nodded.

"Why?"

"I don't know. But I think it has something to do with Leah Oliver's death."

Leah clutched her chest. Her death? *Her death?* Yes. It was true. Klaus was there. She remembered now. She was lying on the cement, dying, as he walked away. "Oh my God!" she shouted, sending a gust of wind whipping through the office. "It *was* his fault! It was!"

"And I'm afraid he's going to try again," Matt said warily.

"What?! Try what again?" Leah screamed. "I'm dead!"

"And his next attempt..."

"Oh my God, you mean his life! *His* life! Why? Why would he do that? I'm already dead! What is killing himself going to do? Bring me back!"

"I believe he's hiding something. Something that..."

"No!" Leah didn't want to hear anymore, she couldn't, and fled through the wall, leaving the room in a dusty swirl, with ornaments and windows quaking as everyone shielded their eyes.

"Noooooooooo!!!!"

Outside, her cries tore though the snow-covered trees, snapping branches and breaking limbs, her rage aimed at the sky. "Damn you! What kind of God are you anyway? Why are you doing this? What for? Do you want revenge? Is that what you want? Revenge?"

The clouds darkened.

"That's it, isn't it?" she screamed. "I don't believe this! You *want* revenge! This is pathetic! You want revenge for a life you never cared about! Where were you when I needed you?" She swung around, searching the heavens. "Tell me! Where were you then?"

Her cries turned to sobs, and slumping to the ground then, she relived her death. A lonely death. A lonely life. "One word," she said. "Just one. A sign. Anything to let me know you were there. Just one."

A thin ray of light penetrating the clouds as she said this brought additional tears to her eyes. "You're too late. You hear me? You're too late. I've been afraid all my life. Afraid of what I'd done wrong, afraid to love, afraid to care. Afraid of everything. And you allowed it. You allowed my birth and you allowed my death. Only I never lived. Do you hear me? I *never lived.* Had you been there, you would know that. So your revenge means nothing to me. Nothing. Nothing at all. You hear me? Nothing. I don't need it. I don't want it. Go give it to somebody else."

Matt was summoned to the hospital by a frantic floor nurse, and arrived to find Klaus in a straightjacket and foaming at the mouth.

"I need some sleep!" he spat. "Give me something!"

Matt sighed, shaking his head. With that, Klaus started twisting and turning, fighting his restraints. "I said give me something to sleep!"

"Why?"

"Because I need some rest, goddamn it! Why else?"

"I don't know. You tell me."

"You're a quack!" Klaus slobbered, mocking him, *"You tell me!"*

The nurses looked on anxiously, but Matt remained unruffled, even when Klaus started bucking up and down and banging the bed into the wall.

"Let me go! Get me out of this!"

"What's eating at you, Klaus? Talk to me."

Klaus's eyes widened.

"What are you in here for?"

"For rest, you son of a bitch, I told you! I need some rest!"

Matt nodded, his only response to that, a nod. And this sent Klaus into an added rage, where he chewed on one wrist and then the other, slobbering and grunting, trying to get free. Matt motioned for the nurses to leave the room.

"I hate you!" Klaus hissed at Matt, as the door closed behind them. "I hate you! I hate you! I hate you!"

"Obviously," Matt said. "I can see that."

What he really saw though, was a man fighting his own demons and getting an erection in the process, one that protruded from under the sheet.

"I agree, you do need some rest though."

"What?" Hope flickered in Klaus's eyes. "Yes, you're right. I do. I need some rest. Give me something. Are you going to give me something?"

Matt shook his head. He couldn't. "Your system is still..."

"Fuck my system! I need some help! Don't you see? I can't sleep! I can't rest!"

"Since when?"

"What difference does it make?"

"A lot."

Klaus's erection built higher and higher.

"Has it been since Leah died?"

"Yes!" Klaus said. "Yes!"

That came as no surprise. But, "Why?"

"Because! Because she won't let me! She's making me pay!"

"For what?"

Klaus started rocking in his bed, trying to roll onto his stomach so he could gratify himself, his eyes glazing over. Matt walked to the window. "Are you sure it's Leah that's keeping you awake?"

"Yes! Who else?"

Matt kept his back to him. "I don't know. Maybe your father."

"My father?!" Klaus rocked and rocked. "My father?!" He rocked sideways, he rocked up and down. "Look at me! Look at me, you son of a bitch. Look at what you've done to me!"

Matt refused.

"Look at me, I said! You can't turn your back on me! I'm your son! I'm a man! Look!"

Matt faced him with a heavy sigh. "I haven't turned my back on you, Klaus. I'm not your father. Your father is dead, and so is Leah."

Klaus could rock and rock forever. To no end. Reduced to tears of frustration, he tried again and again until all his strength was gone, then just lay there, shrinking and crying, begging to be untied. "Please..."

"I'd like to, Klaus. But where would you go?"

"To sleep," he said. "I just want to go to sleep."

Bethann spent hours composing a dedication to Leah, and when finished, brought it downstairs in a sealed envelope. Richard was going to have it printed on a plaque for the party, but until then, she wanted its contents kept a secret.

"All done?"

She nodded and sat down next to her mom on the couch. "Do you th-think it'll be r-r-ready in time?"

Richard smiled, assuring her it would. "I promise." There was a knock on the door then, and Shad trailed after him as he went to answer it.

It was Matt. "I think I should just move in," he said.

Richard laughed and started toward the den, but Matt motioned to the kitchen, and that's where they would talk.

Klaus had Matt more than worried. Much more.

"You mean, you don't think he's going to make it?" Richard asked.

Matt glanced over his shoulder, not wanting to be overheard. Christine yes, Bethann no. Not Bethann. Let her be innocent a little while longer.

"Remember what I said about the Coroner's report and how I thought Klaus was involved somehow?"

Richard nodded. Of course he remembered. Who could forget?

"Well," Matt said. "I think now more than ever, I was right."

Richard swallowed. "You mean...?"

"Yes," Matt said. "I think he killed her."

-Twenty-

WHETHER OR NOT Klaus actually did kill Leah, would not be a mystery much longer. The following day, Matt phoned Richard at his office, asking him to meet him at the hospital, and together they walked into his room.

Klaus wanted to confess. He wanted to get it off his chest. He couldn't stand it anymore. The tremendous guilt. Only what he had to say, hurt more than they could ever have imagined. He hadn't struck her, hence no bruises. He hadn't laid a finger on her.

"I told her to beg," he said, with tears in his swollen eyes. "I told her to get down on her knees and beg."

"What?" Richard could have hit him, even as the man lay in bed, bandaged, oozing, and crying remorsefully. He even took a step toward him with clenched fists, and it was Matt who held him back.

"Don't!" he said, getting him to make eye contact. "Don't!" Besides, Klaus wasn't finished. There was more.

"I went to help her up then, but she wouldn't let me. She pushed me away. That's when I called her a bastard! I told her she was born a bastard and would die a bastard! A motherless bastard! And that nobody would care!"

Matt and Richard stood there stunned.

"That's when she grabbed her chest. She grabbed it and started screaming at me to get out of her sight! That she couldn't stand the sight of me! What kind of man was I she screamed!"

Matt swallowed. "And you left?"

Klaus covered his face and nodded. "Yes! I did! But I didn't know she was going to die! I didn't! I thought..." He sobbed into his bandaged hands. "I didn't know!"

Richard felt like he was going to throw up, and walked over to the window to focus on something, anything. The parking lot, the cars, the medical building next door. Anything but Klaus.

Matt remained at Klaus's side. It was his job, his duty, and later, when Klaus had run down and they'd left, he and Richard talked in the cafeteria.

"He destroyed her. He literally destroyed her," Richard said. "She was hanging by a thread and he goes and hits her with..."

"No parents," Matt said.

Richard stared into his coffee, and shook his head. "You were right, Matt. She died of a broken heart. And maybe, just maybe, if he'd gone back to help her..."

"Maybe," Matt said. "And that right there is what's eating at him. It's what's been following him around."

Richard's eyes clouded with tears. "But to ask her to beg. Jesus Christ, Matt. Her dignity was all she had left. And to ask her to..."

Matt touched his arm, it was over, there was nothing they could do about it.

Richard pulled away. "So now what? He confesses, gets some rest, and we all go on with our lives like nothing happened?"

Matt smiled sadly. He could understand Richard's sarcasm. But at the same time. "I think it's a misconception," he said. "Confessing and then feeling better. I think you have to come to terms with something, and as part of that healing, then confess."

Klaus had told them he'd had a dream the night before, where Leah wasn't coming to get him anymore, but was pushing him away.

"Are you referring to that so-called *vision* of his?"

Matt nodded. Klaus also told them that he thought the dream meant that Leah had forgiven him. That he prayed that was what it meant.

"You mean, you agree?" Richard asked.

Matt shrugged. "I don't know. But when you think about Leah's reaction yesterday when she heard about his attempted suicide, and how upset she got..."

Richard raised an eyebrow. "Upset? That seemed more like anger to me."

Matt held up two fingers and pressed them together. "Emotions," he said. "Sometimes they're so close, you can't tell one from the other."

Richard sat back and looked around the cafeteria. He knew what Matt was trying to say, and yet. "Yeah, well...he could be lying. Who's to say he even had a dream? Haven't you ever had a patient who lied about something like that?"

Matt nodded. "Yes. Fortunately though, it usually comes out in the end."

Richard sighed, and for a moment, they were quiet. Someone had walked by them with a tray, and the smell reminded Richard of *his* stay here. The food. The sounds. The pain.

"How do you do it, Matt?"

"What?"

"This." Richard held his hands out. "Every day of your life."

Matt smiled. "I'm no saint. There's times when I'd like to walk away. Times like today."

"But you don't."

"I can't," Matt said. "I signed up for the whole run, wire to wire. It's a marathon."

Richard smiled.

"Besides. If we can turn our backs on Klaus, we can turn our backs on anyone. And then one day, who'll be there for us?"

Richard, Christine, and Bethann were the first to arrive at Maple Dale on Christmas Eve. They plugged in all the lights, lit all the candles, and had just started putting out the food when Christine had to rush into the ladies room. This was the third time today she'd felt sick to her stomach, and was so pale when she emerged, Richard asked if she was feeling all right.

"Fine," she said, and promptly started to cry.

Richard put his arms around her. "Christine..."

"I'm fine, really."

"Then why are you crying?"

"I don't know."

Richard laughed softly and glanced at Bethann. When she shrugged, having no idea, he asked again. "Come on, what's the matter?"

Christine sniffed and wiped her nose. "It's nothing really. I just think I'm pregnant."

Richard smiled. "I thought so."

"You mean you knew?" Christine searched his eyes.

"Yes." Richard nodded and kissed her gently. "We've been through this before, remember."

"I remember." They gazed into each other's eyes a moment, then turned instinctively to Bethann, who was smiling, beaming actually, but with tears in her eyes as well.

Leah watched them from the sanctuary of her corner, feeling included somehow, a member of the family, and smiled when Bill came through the doorway.

"I'm sorry," he said, taking one glance and turning to leave.

"No, stay," Richard said. "It's all right."

"No, it's not," Bill told him. "I don't want to see anyone crying on Christmas Eve. Enough is enough."

Christine laughed and dabbed at her eyes. "All right, then I'll stop."

"Good," Bill said.

With this, Bethann proudly announced, "Mom's pregnant." And just like that, Bill got choked up.

"Well, I'll be..." he said, which was all he could say for a second or two. He shook Richard's hand. "Aren't you a little old for this?"

Richard laughed and smacked him on the arm, the way men do, and Bill turned to Christine. "Congratulations," he said, and the two of them just looked at one another at first, then hugged, a gentle embrace. And when they parted, Christine had to dab at her eyes again.

"All right, no more. No more tears."

Walter came in and was given the news. His family, and then Matt and his family arrived shortly after that. As their voices and laughter grew louder, filling the room, Bethann walked over to the arena window. The Christmas lights reflected in the glass, sparkling, as she stared out. They were all talking about Klaus now, and the progress he was making toward a recovery. She wished there was a way she could tell Leah, to let her know.

Leah moved closer. "Oh, Bethann..." she whispered, in a feather of a voice. "You are such a joy to me, you have no idea."

Bethann felt a wave of warmth come over her, and remained perfectly still in an effort to hold onto it.

"It's all right," Leah said softly. "It's all right."

'But I've been so worried about you.'

"Don't be. I'm okay."

Bethann's eyes welled up with tears.

"Don't," Leah said. "Don't be sad. Not for me." She touched Bethann's hair lightly. "I'm finding peace with myself. And I'm finally sharing."

Bethann felt a gentle touch on the side of her face, as a spicy scent embraced her, holding her dear.

"And even though I'm gone, I'll never be far away."

The rest of Leah's Tuesday students and their families arrived. Bethann had invited them. John Smith and his wife came also. He said he was honored to have been included. When everyone was assembled and seated, the dedication began.

Richard, with Bethann at his side, spoke with immense pride. "The idea of an Equestrian Community came about because of Leah Oliver and the love she had for her students and the equestrian program. Therefore, what is being presented to you today." He paused, focusing on the model. "Is given in her memory, and in the memory of Klaus Bukener Sr."

Leah's eyes filled with wonder.

"It is our belief, that if Leah were alive today, she would be able to see in this, the love and gratitude of those whose lives she touched."

Everyone was smiling, everyone was nodding, and all for her. Leah couldn't believe it. *For her.* She hardly knew most of the people, some were even strangers. And yet...

"It is also our belief, that if she were alive today, she would see the true sense of the community theme." Richard motioned for Christine to uncover the plaque, and hesitated then, his voice cracking as he read the inscription out loud.

THE MAPLE DALE EQUESTRIAN COMMUNITY
RIDING ARENA, BARNS, AND CROSS COUNTRY COURSE ARE
GIVEN IN MEMORY OF LEAH OLIVER. BECAUSE OF HER,
THERE WILL ALWAYS BE HORSES AT MAPLE DALE.
THERE WILL ALWAYS BE EQUESTRIANS.
SHE WILL NEVER BE FORGOTTEN.
WITH LOVE,
BETHANN MORRISON

Leah held her breath in awe, this was such an honor. But there was more. Richard raised the plaque higher and read the inscription on the bottom.

> LEAH OLIVER DIED ON AUGUST 14, 1988 AT THE AGE OF THIRTY SEVEN. PRECEDING HER IN DEATH WAS HER MOTHER EVELYN, HER FATHER DANIEL, AND HER SISTER NATASHA. MAY GOD BE WITH THEM. MAY SHE BE AT PEACE.

Everyone stood and applauded, with not a dry eye in the house, as the saying goes, then milled around for a closer look and to read the dedication themselves. Leah wanted to come closer too, but stayed back, and searched out the faces of those she'd come to know and care about.

"Oh, Bill," she whispered. "Did you hear? My mother's name is Evelyn. Evelyn." She smiled at Richard and Christine. "My father's name is Daniel." Matt and Walter were standing next to them. Bethann was laughing with her friends. "My sister's name is Natasha. Natasha. What a beautiful name."

She wanted to say all their names over and over, to shout them to the heavens. And hurrying outside lest she be heard, she danced around in the snow like a ballerina. Singing and dancing, and twirling and twirling.

Snowflakes melted as they lit upon her, twisting and turning, glittering as she danced farther and farther away. Then something, a thought, a recent memory, made her stop and look back. She could see everyone clearly, so very clearly. The building was bursting with joy, with lights, with love. She closed her eyes and in the distance could hear the horses, the sounds of their hooves hitting the ground, and the sounds of the student's laughter. The students. She hadn't abandoned them after all. And Bethann, dear sweet Bethann, had found a way for her to always be with them.

"Thank God!" she whispered. "Thank God!"

There was no one to hear her, no one to say I understand, no ray of light, it was pitch black. Yet, she didn't feel alone. Not anymore. She felt as if someone was listening. Someone who cared, and she raised her eyes to the sky.

"Thank You!" she said. "Thank You for all of this!"

The thick clouds separated, showing the stars above, tiny little specks miles and miles away, and yet so close, she raised her arms to see if they held any warmth.

They brightened, the brightness was hers, and she could see, really see for the first time. It had been there all along. Always.

She raised her arms higher, wanting to experience even more, to know everything, to finally move on, and smiled when someone reached down to show her the way. After all these years, a lifetime, Leah still recognized her. "Mother," she said, and felt the tender warmth of her loving touch.

Christmas Eve, 1988, Leah Oliver disappeared.

An equestrian, horse trainer, and environmentalist, MaryAnn Myers lives with her family in northeast Ohio, and is currently working on her sixth novel, *The Frog, the Wizard, and the Shrew.*